MONSTER PETS: DRACULA'S CAT

BOOK 1 OF THE MONSTER PET ADVENTURES

BY GARY BUETTNER

Copyright © 2014 Gary Buettner

Second Edition
ISBN: 978-0692697740
Print Edition

Published by Masked Planet

Cover design by Brian P. Easton
Original art by Chris Monroe
Monster Pets logo by Eryck Webb Graphics

All Rights Reserved.
No portion of this publication may be reproduced, stored in any electronic system, or transmitted in form or by any means, electronic, mechanical, photocopy, recording or otherwise, without written permission from the authors. This is a work of fiction. Any resemblance to any actual person, living or dead, events or locales is entirely coincidental.

For my four little monsters…
Mina, Sean, Abby and
Grayson…

BOOK 1 OF

DRACULA'S CAT

DRACULA

BELFRY (THE CAT)

1
IT CAME IN THE MAILBOX

As soon as Mina saw the large, tiger-striped envelope, she knew exactly what it was. She had been stalking the mailman for months and checking the mailbox twice a day. Finally!

Mina hopped up and down in the kitchen as she tore it open. It was a brochure for the coolest summer camp ever—Zoo Camp! A summer spent swimming with the dolphins, feeding tigers and running with zebras. Her heart practically jumped out of her chest as her imagination ran wild envisioning possibilities. It was only autumn, but it's never too soon to start planning for summer vacation. When it came to getting into a good summer camp, the fastest cheetah caught the gazelle. If there was something that Mina loved more than adventure, it was animals and Zoo Camp offered both.

Mina's mother giggled at Mina's craziness. "Looks like fun". Her mother was a chef and cooked the best food ever.

She was cooking right then and the smells coming from the kitchen were making Mina's mouth water. Vegetarian taco night! Mina didn't like the sound of her voice, though. It was saying *fun,* but was sounding like *forget it.* "You'll have to talk to your father."

Mina's father's office was down the hall and she got there in three bounces. She knocked, but pushed the door open before getting an answer. "Daddy?"

She heard a sneeze from beneath a pile of old papers rolled into tubes. They looked like the ancient Egyptian scrolls they had seen at the museum.

"Dad, did you steal these from the museum?" Mina laughed. Her Dad was an accountant not a cat burglar, although he was much cooler than your average accountant.

"The Mummy hasn't filed taxes for three-thousand years," he said, knocking over a pile of dusty scrolls. Mina's dad exploded in a flurry of sneezes. "Now, he wants to pay for them with cursed artifacts."

Mina's dad wasn't joking—he was an accountant for monsters. He kept track of money for mummies, vaults for vampires and zeroes for zombies.

She didn't get to see many actual monsters, though, which was too bad. Her dad usually went to the monsters' houses but it looked like he was working from home tonight (maybe the mummies didn't have the internet—

one never knew). Her dad's client list was pretty cool, though it had earned her the nickname *Monster Mina* at school and she could probably live without that.

Mina held the Zoo Camp brochure behind her back. "Can I talk to you about something?"

"Sure thing, sweetie," he said, taking off his glasses and rubbing his eyes. He returned his thick-framed glasses to his eyes. "As long as this isn't about another summer camp."

Her shoulders slumped. This was going to be harder than she thought… "Daddy!"

"I'm sorry, but you've been kicked out of every summer camp in the tri-state area."

"This one is different, though."

"They're all *different*, honey: Astronomy camp, gymnastics camp, bike racing camp. Do you remember circus camp? That clown will never be the same."

"That was…an accident. This will be different. I promise."

He sighed. "Let me see."

She handed over the brochure. On the cover, a tiger was pouncing, claws bared, fangs flashing. She quickly flipped it over before her dad saw. On the other side, though a great white shark stalked the ocean, eyes black, and teeth like big white kitchen knives.

Her dad read the brochure, but it was taking him way

too long.

"They have tigers and pythons and hyenas and sharks and…"

"Honey, you got into a fight with a clown, I can only imagine what you would do with a tiger."

"I beat the clown. Doesn't that count for anything?"

"Honey…," Mina's dad said, in his *get-ready-for-bad-news* voice.

"Daddy, please, I want this more than I ever wanted anything, ever. I want to work with animals and take care of them. I think I might want to be a vet.

Mina loved animals and if it had been up to her, the entire house would have been a giant animal sanctuary with rabbits in the garage, sheep in the yard and ducks in the bathtub, but her father was allergic to every creature that crawled on the earth, swam in the sea or flew in the sky. "This is my *density*."

"Destiny," her dad corrected.

"I know. I was trying to be cute."

"That was pretty cute." Her dad took a deep breath, held it forever, and let it out. "How much does it cost?" He flipped it over, read the fine print on the back page. "Ungh," he said. That was a bad sound, worse than the *getting-ready-to-give-bad-news* voice. "*That* would cost a lot of cursed artifacts." He shook his head. "I'm sorry, honey, too dangerous…"

"I'll be extra, super carefully safe."

"Too dangerous for *my wallet*. How about math camp?"

Mina trudged back down the hall.

That night, even her mom's tacos had no flavor.

2
LAZERS

THE NEXT DAY was hot dog day at school, but Mina considered hot dogs the Frankenstein's monsters of the food world and she wrinkled her nose at the creature feature on her tray. The cafeteria at her school didn't really cater to vegetarians, so Mina got a big, juicy apple, a milk and joined her only two friends at the table they had already staked out.

Mina and her friends were seventh graders at Archer's Landing Junior High School.

"Hi Mina," Rex said. "Ready for another exciting school year?" Her friend Rex greeted her as she got to their table. He hid behind long, dark bangs that hung over his eyes like a veil. He wore black jeans, black sneakers and a black hoody. He cradled a duct-taped skateboard like an infant.

"You are *sooo* funny…" Mina said. "…looking." Rex got as much grief for how he looked as Mina did for her father's job. Actually, he was kind of cute, but he *knew* it and was always looking in the mirror, so that effectively canceled out the effect of his cuteness. Anyway, he didn't seem too interested in making friends with anyone but Mina, even though he didn't *act* like it. Her mother told her that sometimes boys teased girls they secretly liked. Mina blushed. She didn't really think he was in love with her or anything. Not like that.

"Two words," said Vanessa, the third person at the table and Mina's best friend: "Zoo. Camp." She held up her own brochure.

After talking to her dad last night, the tiger on the brochure seemed to be pouncing on Mina's dreams, ready to tear them to shreds with its claws. "Maybe we can be roomies!" She brushed her long red hair out of her eyes.

"Slim chance. Can't go," Mina said, dropping into a seat.

"Why?!"

"Too dangerous. Too expensive," She said and took a bite out of her apple. She didn't want to talk about it anymore.

"Sucks," Vanessa said. She wore a shirt with a galloping horse on it. It seemed like every article of clothing she owned had some kind of horse on it. Her family was kind of rich and they had their own horse farm. Mina consid-ered herself lucky to have her own bicycle; Vanessa had her own horse and her own bathroom.

"Parents always say *dangerous* when they mean *expensive*," Rex said. "When I broke my skateboard, my parents said it was too dangerous to get another one."

Mina almost choked on the apple. "You told us that you broke your skateboard jumping off the roof of your house…"

"Yeah, so? It was extremely cool."

Vanessa nodded. "It was cool, you have to admit. Even though you could have broken your neck."

Mina rolled her eyes, then something occurred to her.

"Wait—if your parents wouldn't buy you a new board, how did you get this one?"

Rex shrugged, "I mowed lawns all summer and saved up enough."

"I babysit sometimes," Vanessa said. Her parents were rich and money wasn't ever a problem for her, but Mina appreciated the input nonetheless.

"*I* could babysit," Mina said and crunched her apple.

Vanessa wrinkled her nose.

"What?" Mina was talking around a mouthful of apple.

"You don't have any brothers or sisters," she said. "You don't really know anything about taking care of little kids."

Mina shrugged. "How hard could it be?"

Now, Vanessa rolled her eyes. "You have *no* idea."

"I think you're missing an obvious thing here…" Rex

said.

"What?"

"Why do you want to go to Zoo Camp?"

"Because it's awesome and I want to learn to take care of animals."

"Taking care of animals? Well, then?"

"Well, *what*?"

The bell rang. Rex sprang from his seat and smiled. "Oh, nothing. I just might have a great idea for you is all." Then he walked away.

Later that afternoon during math class, Mina stared out the window. Across the street, a woman was walking six dogs at once. The leashes were knotted together and it looked like she was about to fall and be dragged down the street. *She needs help*, Mina thought, *I wonder who she would call...* "Oh," she said out loud.

The entire class turned and stared at her.

That lady would probably gladly pay somebody to help walk all those dogs, and to feed them and take care of them... A pet sitter!

Mina turned back to the class and noticed that all eyes were on her.

"Uh," she sputtered. "This, uh, math all makes sense now."

"It's only the ninth day of school and *Monster Mina* is already acting like a freak!" The class erupted with laughter. Silvia gave a wicked smirk, pleased with the response to her comment. Silvia was the smartest girl in school, which would not have meant all that much, but she was also the prettiest and most popular. On top of all of that, she was the meanest, by far.

"Monster Mina does it again." This brought another eruption.

Mina slunk down in her seat.

"Silvia!"

Mrs. Gretch, their teacher, had evidently been born with no sense of humor or personality of any kind. She never laughed, never smiled, and her classroom was a collection of empty bulletin boards hung over dull, gray walls and an empty desk. Even the cobwebs in the corners seemed bored. But, she would never stand for Silvia's behavior or any students making fun of each other, so at least her class was a safe haven. Excruciatingly dull, but safe.

"I'm sorry, Mrs. Gretch," Silvia said her voice dripping with syrupy sweet sarcasm. "Mina was going to answer that problem and I interrupted her. I apologize." She turned in her seat to face Mina and whispered, "Go ahead, Mina, what was the answer?"

"Uh," Mina said. She knew this stuff. She knew it. She looked at the board, trying to find the right problem to answer, but her attention kept being pulled back to Silvia's face like a magnet. "Uh, the answer is, uh…" Mina wanted her desk to open up and swallow her. "I don't know."

"Two-thousand, four-hundred and fifty-six," Silvia said, without even taking her eyes off Mina.

The bell rang and Mina was saved for now, but next came gym class and that could be a real disaster.

🐾 🐾 🐾 🐾 🐾

HER BAD MOOD had crept into her every thought and Mina decided that the pet sitting idea was stupid. She would never be able to make it work and she doubted that people would pay her to take care of their animals, anyway. She was never going to Zoo Camp and it was time she got used to it.

Coach Julie, the gym teacher, was the shortest adult Mina had ever seen. Nevertheless, she started the school year with basketball. "C'mon, people up and down the court, don't be a loser!" Mina was thankful that she didn't get stuck on Silvia's team, though she was disappointed to see Vanessa had.

Rex lounged on the bench next to her. They watched Silvia owning the court with the grace of a pro-athlete.

"You ever notice when you're too good at something, then you're a geek?" Mina said. "But if you're not good enough at something, then you're a loser. And if you try too hard, you're a wannabe." She rested her chin in her hand. "So how does she get away with *everything*?" It was true. Silvia was the head cheerleader, captain of the girls' basketball team and the president of more clubs than Mina even knew existed; almost as if the school made up clubs just for her to be the president of.

"She doesn't even have to try—she's just good at everything. She just *is*."

"I don't think she even sweats," Mina said, wiping sweat from her own brow.

"Perfection sucks. That's why I neither try, nor care."

"Ahh, the rally-cry of the lazy loser."

"I prefer the term *lazer*."

"Lazer?"

"Lazy plus loser equals lazer. I think I might make t-shirts."

"Put me down for one," Vanessa said, flopping onto the bench next to the other two. "Silvia has me beat."

"Wait, you were on *her* team."

"Yeah, she stole the ball from me."

Silvia dribbled the ball slowly down the court, giving the evil-eye to anyone who looked like they might try to block her or steal the ball, even the players on her own team. Those players mostly crossed their arms and rolled their eyes.

"They don't even try," Mina said, thinking of that defeated feeling she felt in math class.

"More lazers," Vanessa said.

"Join the *lazer revolution*," Rex said.

Silvia stopped at half court and effortlessly sunk a shot; nothing but net.

It was the other team's turn to have the ball, but they just milled around like extras in a zombie movie.

"I've had enough," Mina said, hopping up from the bench. She marched across the court, scooped up the basketball and dribbled toward the other basket, directly towards Silvia.

None of the other team moved, but Mina didn't care.

"Monster Mina strikes again," Silvia said.

"Monster…monster…," the chant picked up, led by Rex. Vanessa chanted, too, stomping her feet on the floor.

Mina glanced at the crowd and realized they weren't making fun of her, they were cheering for her. Cheering for somebody to stand up to Silvia…

Silvia saw it too. The surprised expression melted into boiling anger. She dropped into a defensive position, her hands up like claws. "Bring it!" she growled.

"Monster! Monster!"

Mina stopped short, stood and dropped the ball at Silvia's feet like she didn't even care. "Silvia the *Wannabe*."

The bleachers went crazy—they couldn't have roared louder if Mina had dunked the ball.

The bell rang and everyone left to change, leaving Silvia standing alone on the court.

HER OUTLOOK ON life greatly improved, Mina stopped by the computer lab after class and made a flyer:

MINA'S PET SITTING
No Animal Too Big!
No Job Too Small!

Mina put her cellphone number at the bottom and then printed out a bunch. She skipped the bus and walked home, sticking them up on every phone pole from her school to her house, and when she got home, she sat at the kitchen table and stared at her phone.

After the first half hour, her mother stopped at the table. "Are you waiting for a call? Maybe from a *boy*?"

"Gross," she said. "Only if he has a dog that needs walking." Though, Rex wasn't actually *gross*, but the thought of talking to him on the phone made her feel a little woozy, even though she talked to him in person every day. She brought her attention back to the phone.

It did not ring.

3
MIDNIGHT VILLAS

After dinner, Mina's dad asked her if she wanted to take a ride with him. Mina perked up. The Mummy's taxes were done and he had to drive to Midnight Villas to drop them off. She was excited because she had never been to the monster neighborhood before, but what he said next made it even better, "Bring a couple fliers so we can hang them up on the way."

Mina didn't say a word. She just grabbed up her phone, the stack of fliers and hurried out to the car.

They drove for a while in silence before her father spoke. "I really respect what you're trying to do with the pet-sitter idea," her Dad said. "If you can earn enough money to go, you have my permission."

"Thanks," Mina said, staring at her phone.

They stopped to hang flyers along the way and she was almost out when it started to get dark and the streetlights began to flicker to life.

"Here we are," he said. "Midnight Villas. Lock your doors. Oh, and do me a favor—don't put up any flyers here, okay?" He laughed nervously. "Now, hold my hand."

He explained that Midnight Villas was protected by a spell cast by the Voodoo Queen—No one could enter the neighborhood without being invited, kinda the same way vampires couldn't come into your house unless you invited them in. Her dad had a standing invitation to the Villas, and if you held hands with someone who was invited you were allowed to enter.

They passed through the gates, both of them shivering as they drove through the spell.

Mina pressed her face up against the window.

Bare skeletal trees lined the crooked streets of Midnight Villas. The houses leaned to one side or threatened to collapse completely and cracked and crumbling gravestones filled the yards. The place was a mash-up of a dozen different nightmares. A UFO, silver and glowing faintly green, sat crashed next door to an ancient Egyptian pyramid that dominated the street. In the distance, Mina could make out the mast and sails of a massive ship that flew the skull and crossbones above its decks, and even though there was no ocean in Archer's Landing, she could smell the salt air and hear sea gulls.

Above it all, sat Count Dracula's castle, stuck into a hillside like a rotten tooth in a dead man's mouth.

"This is the coolest place I've ever seen," Mina said. "I've never seen so many castles before," she said, amazed at the houses they passed and forgetting her phone for a minute. "Is that… a spaceship?"

"Yup. Alien family. Nice folks, too."

They passed a particularly creepy looking house that felt like it was staring back at them, watching as they passed. Mina's dad sped up just a bit.

"Scary," Mina said.

"Yeah," her dad said. "That's the one house that even scares monsters. I don't think anybody lives there. I mean, well, you know what I mean."

"I can't imagine who would want to."

"Haunted houses usually go for big money in this neighborhood, but that house is, I don't know, *extra* haunted somehow."

"Haunted? Like, ghosts?"

"I've met a couple of ghosts, so no, not like that. It's like *fear itself* lives there."

She turned around to keep looking at it and still had the feeling that it was looking at her. The walls were crooked and the roof drooped, all ready to fall in on anyone unlucky enough to be caught inside. The ground was cracked and crumbling around it, ready to swallow the place whole. Mina shook her head. She had seen cozier-looking dumpsters. The place wasn't so much creepy-cool or spooky; it looked really dangerous, like a rusty nail waiting to be stepped on.

Her dad pulled the car into the sandy driveway of the enormous pyramid.

"Okay, stay in the car and I'll be right back." He got out and walked up the sandy path.

Mina went back to focusing on her phone, wishing it to ring A shadow suddenly moved outside her window and she popped her head up to see a big black dog outside the car. It was just standing there, staring at her. She waved at it and wished that she had a treat. She knew she was supposed to stay in the car, but was about to get out anyway when the dog turned and wandered off. Mina watched it go, worried that it was lost and hungry, when she noticed a light pole on the sidewalk. A flyer was posted offering a *gently* used coffin for sale. All the little phone number tabs had been torn off.

"Ick," she said. In the darkening sky, a colony of giant bats took to the night, almost blotting out the moon. Ground-hugging fog crept out of the woods and swirled around the twisting trees and ancient gravestones. Mina shivered and giggled at the same time.

After a few minutes though, she looked back at the pole and the coffin flyer with all the numbers torn off. *That* flyer seemed to have worked very well. She wondered if monsters had pets…

Mina looked to see if her dad was coming. He wasn't.

She looked down at her phone again to see if she had somehow missed a call. She hadn't. She looked back at the pole with the one, lonely flyer, blowing gently in the evening breeze... She crept out of the car, tacked up a flyer just beneath the other one and slipped back into the passenger seat just as her father appeared at the door of the pyramid. He hurried back down to the car. "You okay?"

"Yup."

"You want to get ice cream?"

"I'm not a little kid, Dad."

"Is that a *no* on the ice cream?"

Mina was quiet for a minute. She really didn't want him to notice her flyer... "I, uh, didn't say *no*. I'm just saying I'm not a kid anymore."

"That's my girl."

WHEN THEY GOT home, Mina finished her mint chocolate chip cone and went to work on her homework. She was concentrating on math when her phone suddenly rang. She jumped in her seat and then answered it...

"Is this Mina's Pet Sitting service?"

"Yes, this is Mina. May I ask who is calling?"

"Of course, my dear. I am... Dracula."

4
FREAK OUT MUCH?

"ARE YOU INSANE?" Vanessa hissed in science class the next day. Her safety goggles were lopsided and they made her look like a mad scientist.

"What are we talking about?" Mina was pouring two test tubes together. The red liquid mixed with the blue liquid and turned purple. That proved something, but Mina wasn't sure exactly what.

"We're talking about pet sitting for vampires!" Vanessa said. "Aren't you worried he's going to *bite* you?"

"Not really. He seems really nice. He lives in a castle," Mina said.

"Yeah, you mentioned the vampire's *castle*, but I'm more worried about the vampire's *fangs*," Vanessa said.

"Don't worry so much. You know me."

"Yeah, I know you, that's what I'm worried about." Vanessa gave her an awkward hug.

"And if he does turn me into a vampire, I'm totally

going to bite you."

"I would be so tasty," Vanessa said thoughtfully. "Like a caramel Frappuccino."

"Maybe if we lived forever, we could actually get this chemistry lab done."

"Ladies," Mr. Smith, the science teacher, said. "Less talk. More science." Mr. Smith was Silvia Smith's father and she must have gotten her looks from her mother because he was short and chubby. His goggles were lopsided too, but he actually was a scientist and he always seemed mad at them, so Mina figured that the look worked for him.

5
DRACULA'S CAT

MINA RODE HER bike to school the next day so that she could ride to Dracula's castle in Midnight Villas as soon as school was over. Dracula had invited her and said she could pass through the Voodoo Queen's spell. She shivered just the same way as she had the night before.

She had to ride past the Mummy's Pyramid to get there and when she checked her flier, all of the phone number tabs had been taken.

"Yes!" Mina pumped her fist. "Oh, yeah!"

She continued until she saw the mailbox with a bat on it and then rode her bike up the winding driveway until she got to the huge wooden doors. The knocker was almost as big as she was. She managed to get underneath it and force it away from the door. It fell back against the wood with a single, thunderous boom.

Mina wondered if anyone could have missed that noise. She didn't think so, but she waited a long time and no one answered. She was thinking about trying to knock again when the door creaked open.

She didn't see anyone standing inside. "Uh, hello?"

Maybe this was a bad idea.

"Please enter." The voice seemed to float out of the darkness. Or maybe the darkness itself was talking, Mina wasn't sure.

She took a deep breath, gathered her courage and stepped inside. She blinked trying to make her eyes get used to the dark inside.

It was hard to know where the shadows ended and the building began. The windows were sheathed in heavy black curtains to keep out the sunlight. The furniture, all wood and iron, seemed better suited for a torture chamber than a living room.

She squinted at a nearby chair that was lined with rusty, metal spikes. She hoped that he wouldn't offer her a seat. Above her, creepy paintings glared down from the walls like the ghosts of hanged men.

The darkness came toward her, a shadow within a shadow.

"Welcome to my home," the voice continued.

Something rubbed against her leg and she jumped. But it was only a cat. A cat! She reached down and petted it. "Nice kitty," she said, not taking her eyes off the moving shadow.

"No, he's not particularly," the voice said. A match struck in the darkness and a candle was lit. The golden light was warm, but shy and it spread only enough light for Mina could see the man in front of her. He seemed as tall as the ceilings in her house and wore an old-style black suit that seemed to be sewn together from shadows. Over the suit, he wore a long black coat instead of the cape she imagined. And, an almost western hat sat on his head. He smiled beneath it, revealing two perfectly white fangs. "I am... Dracula."

Count Dracula? His outfit looked more like *Sheriff* Dracula.

The flame on the candle leapt at the sound of his name.

"You, uh, said that you need someone to take care of your cat?"

"Yes...My cat, Belfry, got into a bit of a scrape with another creature."

"Ouch," Mina said.

"Quite," Dracula said. "He has been cared for by a veterinarian who stitched him up, but now the time has come to have the stitches removed and due to an..." he paused to search for the word, "altercation, between the veterinarian and Belfry, she has refused to come out to the house again. And so, Belfry must to be taken to the vet to have his stitches removed. During *regular business hours*." He spit the last words like they were not at all tasty, even downright grotesque.

"Mr. Dracula," Mina said. The flames of the candle leapt again. "What can I do to help?"

Dracula smiled. "I would like you to take Belfry to the vet to have his stitches removed and return him to the castle. He has an appointment this Saturday *afternoon*." Apparently, *afternoons* were pretty gross, too.

"No problem. I can do that," Mina said. She was startled when the cat leaped into the air, flapped huge black wings and landed on Dracula's shoulder. It licked its paw in a manner most regal.

Dracula's cat has wings, she thought. *Okay, then.*

Mina laughed. It all would have been shocking and scary had the cat not been fitted with white plastic cone around its neck. *That* looked pretty goofy. She had seen animals wearing cones before and knew that they kept the animals from biting their stitches after surgery. She looked back at the cat's face and it seemed that the cat noticed her amusement over the cone. It squinted its green eyes at her in a most evil fashion. She looked away.

"I'll be here Saturday afternoon to take care of Belfry. Thank you for calling me, Mr. Dracula."

The flame leaped again.

When Mina got home, she googled *Midnight Villas*.

She found *Supercreepopedia* and clicked on the listing for the neighborhood.

> *Midnight Villas is a suburban development originally created at the turn of the century by Count Vlad Dracula as a residential area for monsters wishing to do business and reside in comfort.*
>
> *The property expanded from Count Dracula's castle, moved brick-by-brick from Transylvania, to includes such monster luminaries as the Mummy, Frankenstein and the Wolfman. The area is open to all monsters and grows each year.*

Her cell rang.

Vanessa.

She answered the phone as she got up from the bed. "Hey, you."

"Good, you're still alive. I was worried you might be the *Bride of Frankenstein* by now. Spill your guts sister, I want to know what the place is like. Everybody is going to want to know."

"Ha-ha," Mina said humorlessly. "You're so funny it hurts my brain."

"I'm serious! And worried…" Vanessa said. "As cool as they are, there's a reason that the monsters keep away from the rest of us."

"Yeah, for *their own safety*." From what the website

said, it sounded like they were looking for a place where they could be happy and safe. She couldn't blame them. "I told you not to worry. Oh, hey wait, I have another call, hold on." Mina put Vanessa on hold and answered the other call. "Hello?"

"May I speak to Mina of Mina's Pet Sitting?" The voice sounded old, really old, like practically ancient. It seemed to echo from a great distance away.

"This is Mina. May I ask with whom am I speaking?"

"I am the Pharaoh Amon-Ra," he said, and when he didn't get the response he was expecting, he added with an annoyed sigh, "*The Mummy.*"

"Oh," Mina said, feeling a little stupid. "You need a pet sitter?"

"Yes, for my cobra."

"Your cobra? Yes, I'm available. I'd love to take care of your, uh, cobra." She found a pen and wrote down the important information. "Okay, I'm looking forward to meeting you. Thank you!" She ended the call and got back to Vanessa. "I got another pet sitting gig!"

"Awesome! Zoo Camp here we come!"

Another call buzzed in on the other line. "I'm getting another call! I'll hit you back later, okay?"

"Good luck!"

Mina answered the call and spoke with the Wolfman's

wife. As soon as she was finished, the phone rang again and didn't stop ringing for the rest of the evening. Mina danced around her room as she talked to monster after monster, making appointments and getting closer to Zoo Camp with every call.

6
THE FOREST

MINA ROLLED UP to Castle Dracula in the early afternoon. She had put a couple of soft, cozy blankets in the basket on the front of her bicycle for the cat to ride in and one to cover him up as the forecast promised sunny weather all day.

A note hung on the door, written in fancy letters that read simply: *Come in, Mina.* The door swung open easily when she pushed and inside she found the big cat, Belfry, waiting for her. His wings were tight against his sides and she could barely see them. *That should make this easier*, she thought.

"Alright kitty, let's do this," she said, scooping him up and petting the soft fur on top of his head. He fit perfectly in the basket, but it took him a few minutes of kneading and turning to get comfortable. When he was finished, the look he tossed her said *I am now ready to proceed.*

"Okay, your highness," she said. "Here we go!"

Mina coasted down the slope of the driveway only braking when she got to the gate that opened to the street. She looked both ways and was lucky she did because a mini-van was racing toward her.

And not just any mini-van—*it was her dad*!

Panicking, Mina looked around. There was no place to run. She dropped to the ground to hide, as if her bike offered any kind of cover, and pretended to tie her shoe.

After the van passed, she scooted into the street holding her bike up with one hand. Anyone watching would have seen a bike rolling along by its self. And, maybe nobody would notice that sort of thing in this neighborhood.

But the mini-van's brake lights flashed red as it pulled to a stop.

"Oh, crap!" Mina snatched a blanket from beneath Belfry, who screeched in protest, wrapped it around her own head like a scarf, covering her curls.

The mini-van pulled forward and turned down another street, revealing the stop sign Mina hadn't noticed before.

Sort of relieved but still wanting to get out of Midnight Villas as quickly as possible, she looked for a shortcut. Across the street was a wooded area between two houses and the opening of a path between the trees. She aimed her bike that way and pedaled as fast as she could.

The going got tough after she left the street and rocketed into the woods along the path. "Whoa!"

The cat's ears flattened along its head in anger. It gave her a nasty look.

"Hold on, kitty!" she said.

The forest was like no other forest that Mina had ever seen. The trees looked angry and hateful, their clawing branches seemed ready to reach for her like they would like nothing more than to tear her apart. Heck, even the underbrush seemed to conceal terrible secrets and she didn't know if she was more likely to find a dead body in this place or become one.

She pedaled slowly forward. She enjoyed a nature walk as much as the next girl, but there was nothing natural about this piece of ground. She shivered as much from fear as from the chilled shadows beneath the smothering canopy of trees.

She glanced back the way she had come. If she turned around now, she would get caught and this whole thing would be over before it started. She took a deep breath, clutched the handlebars of her bike in a death grip and pushed forward.

They blazed through the woods, dodging fallen trees and large stones half-buried in the ground. Beneath the wide branches of the trees, the forest was dark and deathly silent.

Something moved in the woods beside them and Mina skidded to a stop to listen, but she didn't hear anything.

Could have been the shadows, she thought. On the other hand, it could have been something. In the woods behind Midnight Villas, it definitely could have been something.

Definitely.

Belfry hissed.

Mina stared at the cat. "Is it something bad?"

The cat hissed again, arching its back.

"That's bad enough!" Mina raced away down the path, standing up and pedaling for her life.

A huge beast crashed through the woods, racing after them, branches cracking and snapping as it came.

Mina was in shock, her feet flying and Belfry hissing up a storm. But then something even worse hit them…

Gag! What was that smell?!

Mina desperately wanted to peek back to see what it was, but she had to keep her eyes on the path or her and Belfry would wipe out.

A jagged branch snagged her shirt and tore her from her bike. "Oof!" She hit the ground so hard that it knocked the wind out of her.

Her bike teetered and crashed to the ground.

Unable to unfold his wings in the blanket, the cat hit the ground as hard as Mina had. When he glared back toward her, he saw the creature gaining on them and his eyes grew wide with terror. Belfry arched his spine and hissed like a steam pipe.

Not good! Mina thought.

She scrambled to her feet, grabbing up Belfry without caring that he was hissing and scrambling back to her bike. She plopped Belfry in the basket and jumped on, missing the pedals and skinning her ankle. Ignoring the pain, she managed to stand up on her pedals and pumped her feet with all she had.

The path opened up at a jagged chasm that wound its way through the woods. She tried not to think about how deep it was…or what might be waiting at the bottom.

Mina saw a stone that sloped upward like a ramp. She relaized It was either the ramp or turn and face the creature, so she pedaled faster. *Too bad Rex was going to miss this!*

Mina held her breath as they hit the ramp and went airborne. Behind them, she could hear the creature skid to the edge of the chasm, sending stones and dirt tumbling over the side.

They were going to crash…they were going to crash…they were going to crash…

Mina squinted her eyes, bracing for impact, and they landed hard on the other side of the chasm. The bike wobbled under them and Mina thought she was still going to crash, but she managed to keep it upright. She pedaled until it felt like her heart would explode.

The wood suddenly opened to a paved road and Mina emerged from the forest only a few blocks from downtown. She felt the shiver as she passed out of Midnight Villas' protective spell.

"We're okay!" She grinned at Belfry "But no more shortcuts…"

Belfry licked one paw, unimpressed.

Mina checked the city map on her phone. Her shortcut hadn't taken her far from where she was headed, so she plotted a route and tucked her phone in her pocket. "Okay, Belfry, let's-"

"Mina?" A car had stopped next to the curb.

"Mom?"

Mina covered Belfry with the blanket.

"Hey, Mom!" Mina waved, smiling way too big. She tried to dial it back a little. "Uh, what are you doing down here?"

"I was just going to ask you the same thing. Who's your friend?"

"Oh, pet sitting, ya'know? Taking this cat to the vet for Mr…," Mina caught herself. "Er…," she said. "Mister, uhh, *Mister Acula*." She nodded. Yep. She was smooth…

"Mr. *Acula*?"

Belfry poked his head up out of the basket. Mina pretended to pet him, but was really trying to push him back down in the blankets before he spread his wings. He pushed back against her hand. She ignored him and nodded, still smiling.

"Be careful, honey," Mom said. "Black cats are bad luck."

"Nah," Mina said. "He's a sweetheart."

"Do you want a ride?"

"No!" Her voice was too loud. "I mean, I really want to do this myself. I'll, uh, *appreciate* it more."

"Okay," she said. "I'll see you at home." She pulled away from the curb and in a minute was out of sight. Mina's hands were shaking. She realized she still had the blanket wrapped around her head. She rolled her eyes as she pulled it off and stuffed it back in the bike basket.

Belfry hissed again, but this time Mina saw it was that black dog that she'd seen nosing around Midnight Villas the other day. Not a regular dog, though. Something weird about this one. He wore a fancy red collar. "Oh," she said. "You again."

The dog barked.

Belfry hissed lazily, batting at it with its claws.

The black dog growled at the cat.

"Whoa, guys, play nice!"

The dog barked back so loud that it startled her. "Stop!"

The dog lunged forward, still barking.

Belfry snapped his wings open and sprang into the air. Mina grabbed for him, but he got away from her. Belfry soared off down the street.

"Leave me alone! Get away from me!" Mina's anger flared. She screamed at the dog.

The dog stopped barking. He hung its head and turned away. Mina watched as it padded away. She felt like she should say something. Apologize? It was a dog, after all, he wouldn't understand what she was saying. But…

Mina jumped back on her bike and raced down the street, following the flying cat as it arced through the sky.

7
HERE COMES THE BRIDE

THE KING HOTEL, the tallest and oldest building in town, overlooked Archer's Landing like an actual monarch surveying his kingdom.

The gargoyles perched on its roof glared down at the street with bulging eyes and reaching claws. They looked like they wanted to jump down and snatch up a pedestrian. Belfry looked the same as he dive-bombed a flock of pigeons just outside the entrance.

The pigeons exploded into flight as Belfry crashed into the revolving door so hard that it sent it spinning.

Mina ditched her bike and pushed through the doors, breathless, and was just in time to see the winged cat disappear through a set of doors at the opposite end of the long hall. She sucked in a deep breath and tore down the hall. "Belfry, c'mon...," she said, pulling open the enormous door. "I'll rub your belly!"

The bride and groom were surprised to say the least.

Mina clamped her hand over her mouth. She had no idea they held weddings at The King Hotel.

Every eye in the hall turned to see who was destroying the special day.

Cheeks flushed, she gave a little nervous wave. She was sure everyone could hear her heart pounding in her chest.

Through it all, the priest went on like he had a tight schedule to keep or something. "Dearly beloved…" he said, then clearing his throat to regain everyone's attention.

Belfry cleared his throat. *Ack-gack.*

Mina's eyes shot up to where the winged cat sat on the arch just above the priest's bald head.

He continued, raising his voice a bit with each interruption even though everyone in the hall was fixated on the impossible winged cat. "We are gathered here today…"

Ack-gack.

"…to join this couple…"

Ack-ack-gack!

"…in holy matrimony…"

Ack-ga-gack-gack!

"…oh, for…!" He snatched the bride's bouquet from her and flung it at the cat. For a man of the cloth, he had deadly aim, but Belfry dodged it midair and it came down amid the bridesmaids, who were so eager to catch the flower that they collapsed into a tangled mess of up-do's and taffeta. The girl who caught the bouquet was the one girl who seemed the least interested in pursuing it: Vanessa.

"What are *you* doing here?" Mina was shocked to see her.

Vanessa made a *duh* gesture. "Uh, *wedding*?"

"Oh yeah, right, your cousin's wedding." Mina gestured to herself. "Pet sitting."

"How's that working out for you?" Vanessa stared at the flying cat perched on the top of the wedding cake as it began to lick itself. "Maybe you should have gone for baby sitting after all."

Mina shrugged. "No sweat. We're like a Tom and Jerry cartoon."

"Really? Which one are you?"

"Uh-oh," Mina said as a squadron of groomsmen tackled themselves instead of Belfry and slammed into the table the wedding cake sat upon. Mina raced to the cake as it began to tip—if she could just reach it…

She didn't make it.

The cake fell over and exploded on the floor.

Mina lay on her belly on the floor at the edge of the frosted wreckage. She stood up holding the only part she managed to save: the bride and groom from on top of the cake.

Vanessa's eyes were as big as dinner plates.

Mina handed her the bride and groom. "Congratulations," she said.

On the other side of the hall, Belfry sat mockingly on top of a glistening ice sculpture of an angel.

Running across the room, Mina yanked a tablecloth off one of the tables. Glasses and plates crashed to the floor as she tossed it like a fisherman's net over Belfry, still atop the ice angel.

For a second the statue looked like a ghost under a sheet.

Then Belfry took off and soared across the room, a comet of white tablecloth and black wings. He zoomed right out a door held open by a quick-thinking groomsman.

"Thanks a bunch," Mina said sarcastically as she chased Belfry out into the street.

She skidded to a stop, scanning the busy street, but didn't see the cat.

"Where'd he go?" Vanessa appeared on the sidewalk next to her.

"I don't know," Mina said scanning the rooftops desperately. She saw nothing.

"Vanessa!" The voice boomed from inside the hall.

"Oops. I have to go help my cousin get frosting out of her hair." Vanessa hurried back inside.

A sheet-covered ghost zoomed past. *Belfry!*

Mina ran down the street, chasing him as he soared

ahead of her.

The cat looked back over his shoulders to see Mina gaining on him and flew right into a lamppost. Dazed, he flopped onto the pavement.

Mina caught up to him. "See! That wouldn't have happened if you let me get your stitches out and that ridiculous cone off your neck." Mina scooped the cat up, gently petting his head where he had smacked it.

8
THE DOCTOR WILL SEE YOU NOW

Mina and Belfry sat in the veterinarian's waiting room checking out the other animals and pretending to fit in. Belfry seemed to know when to keep his wings tight against his body.

A man sitting next to them had a large turtle on his lap. Its shell reminded Mina of an Army helmet. The poor thing had a cast on its leg.

A colorful parakeet sat on the shoulder of a man across from them. The bird's sore wing jutted out at a painful angle, but that did not keep it from digging its beak into the man's shirt pocket for birdseed.

A woman with green hair held an enormous snake across her shoulders. A python? It had a large bump in its belly the size of a bowling ball. *What had it eaten?* The bump wiggled. *Gross!* Mina shivered. She loved most animals, but snakes? Not so much. She thought of the Mummy's cobra…

"Belfry," the nurse called.

"C'mon, we're up," Mina said, and carried him into the exam room.

Belfry didn't seem to like the exam room. He moaned deep in his throat as soon as he was placed on the exam table. "Relax," Mina said, petting his head.

"Belfry," Dr. Karen, the veterinarian, groaned as she entered.

Dr. Karen was a tall woman, pretty behind her clunky glasses. Her blond hair pulled into a ponytail. Her arms were spotted with bandages and one large one on her cheek.

"I'm Mina and I'm taking care of Belfry for…" she lowered her voice. "Er, *Dracula*."

Dr. Karen set down the clipboard and pulled on a pair of sterile, latex gloves. They were bright purple. "Well, Dracula must really trust you. He is a man, uh, *vampire* who really loves his cat." She turned her attention to her feline patient. "Okay, Belfry, let's take a look at those sutures, shall we?"

The cat raised its back and hissed. Its wings unfolded from its back.

"Play nice," Mina said, gently rubbing his back between his wings. He folded them back in. "Just…relax."

The cat calmed down.

"Wow," Dr. Karen said. "You're a natural. You ever

think about becoming a vet?"

Smiling broadly, Mina nodded.

Dr. Karen gently removed the sutures with scissors and forceps. She did it slowly and carefully, so that Mina could see what she was doing. Finally, she removed the plastic cone from around the cat's neck. He even rubbed his face on her hand afterward. He purred as she stroked his back and strutted around the table, stretching his wings.

"All done," Dr. Karen said, removing her rubber gloves. "Well, if I know anybody who needs a pet sitter, I'll send them your way. And if you have any questions about becoming a veterinarian, don't be afraid to ask."

"Thanks so much!" Mina said, lifting Belfry off the exam table. The vet visit had actually been pretty easy compared to getting him there.

"Oh, no," Mina said, when they got back to the street. For a second, she thought her bike had been stolen, but then she remembered that she left it back at The King Hotel. She had chased Belfry on foot down the alley. She would have to walk back and get it. "Come on," she said, cuddling Belfry against her as she headed down a grassy area between two building, the way she'd come. She would have Belfry back to Castle Dracula and be home before dinner time. She wondered what her mother was making for dinner. She zoned out a bit while she was walking.

Mina coughed, catching a whiff of that nasty stink

from the woods. Her nose wrinkled even as she started shaking with fear. "Uh, oh." She glanced all around and realized that there were no doors or windows near where she was in the alley between the buildings. No people were anywhere nearby. *Don't freak*, she thought. *Don't freak. Don't freak.*

Belfry hissed. His ears went flat along his head.

"Freak!" she said, and ran.

Her feet slipped in mud and she nearly dropped the cat, but she kept going. Then she hit a puddle and spilled onto the ground, dropping Belfry, who landed gracefully on his feet even without the use of his wings.

Mina got to her feet, but as she raised her head, a giant shadow fell across her and she realized she wasn't alone.

The monster was as big as her parent's mini-van. Eyes as big as dinner plates blinked and stared at her. It raised its enormous arms above its head, claws flashing in the afternoon light. Fangs filled the curved mouth and two twisting horns poked into the air atop its misshaped head.

"Belfry…" Mina said, trying to keep her voice calm. "Run. Fly. Get out of here!" She was defenseless. She grabbed a small rock in her hand. Belfry did not back down. He hissed as his back went up, wings and ears tight against his body.

"Is this what you got into a fight with, Belfry?"

The monster roared, slobbering on the ground.

Mina dropped her rock.

The black dog came out of nowhere barking wildly.

The creature's eyes shifted to the dog. Despite its superior size, the monster retreated a little.

The dog forced it back. It looked over its shoulder at Mina as if to say, "Are you still here?"

"Thanks!" Mina took the hint and ran. Belfry jumped into the air.

Behind her, she could hear the dog barking and the monster roaring. Back on the street, she stopped to catch her breath. Leaning against a brick wall, she coughed. "I think we just barely made it, Belfry. Belfry?"

But the cat was gone.

She checked the trees that lined the streets and the bushes in the park. She got down on her hands and knees and checked the sewers. She wandered Archer's Landing scanning the rooftops. She even went back down the alley where they had encountered the monster. Nothing. No blood or signs that the monster had gotten Belfry or the mysterious black dog.

"This isn't happening," she said. "This can't be happening."

It was getting dark. Dracula would be getting up soon.

9
BAD NEWS

Mina sat on the front steps of Castle Dracula watching the sun die in the sky. Mina's hands shook.

The door creaked open.

"Where...is my cat? Where is Belfry?" Dracula loomed over her. He seemed ten-feet-tall.

"I...I have to tell you something and it isn't good," she said. "I'm so sorry."

After the vet, he got away from me. We were attacked by a, uh, I don't know what it was. All hair and fur and claws and horns. It was horrible.

"An *Unspeakable Horror*," Dracula said, voice hollow. "You would only have upset an Unspeakable if you'd gone in the forest." His lip quivered and it took him a full minute to regain himself. "Is Belfry...dead?"

Swallowing hard, Mina shook her head. "I don't know."

Dracula stood silently. Mina could hear the big old clock in the hallway ticking away the seconds for what seemed like an eternity. "Leave my home and never return."

"I'll find him, I-"

"No!" Dracula snapped and icy waves of cold radiated from him. Mina rubbed her goose-fleshed arms.

"You've...done enough." Dracula went inside and shut the door silently. She wished that he had slammed the door. She wished that he had screamed at her. Something. Anything.

Mina picked up her bicycle.

She heard something from inside the castle. She thought Dracula was calling to her, but when she listened, she could hear the man crying. Mina placed her hand on the door as tears burned her own eyes and waited a moment longer, but then she climbed on her bike and slowly pedaled towards home.

A block away from Castle Dracula, she thought she heard a familiar voice and skidded to a halt.

Silvia?

What was the evil queen of Archer's Landing Middle School doing in Midnight Villas? Who would have invited *her* in?

She saw Silvia getting out of a car in the driveway of one of the strangest looking houses in the whole monster neighborhood. It looked like a gigantic concrete block. Silver pipes and conduits snaked in and out of the structure. Weird futuristic windows dotted the outside and several satellite dishes and antennae poked from the roof.

What in the world?

Silvia checked the mailbox and went inside.

That was definitely her house. A man was with her. Mr. Smith, the science teacher from school. He was her dad. He wore a white lab coat and a pair of silver goggles. A tangle of white hair poked out from his head.

Mina wanted to hide, but she was in shadows, so she doubted that they could see her anyway.

When they had gone inside, Mina pedaled away, hurrying past the dark woods at the edge of the neighborhood.

So, this is what going crazy feels like, she thought.

In one day, she had fought an Unspeakable Horror, lost Count Dracula's cat and made an Earth-shattering discovery.

Silvia Smith was…*a monster*?

On another day, she might have laughed, but not today. How could they have gone all these years without knowing? It seemed impossible.

10
SEARCH ENGINE

"I PROMISE YOU," Vanessa said the next day. "It is not that bad. Whatever it is."

"Oh, it's that bad," Mina said. "Possibly worse."

Vanessa had found Mina in the cafeteria with her head slumped onto the table.

"The doctor is in," Vanessa said, sitting down next to her.

Mina sighed. She didn't even know where to start. "I lost Dracula's cat."

Vanessa smiled, waiting for the punchline and when she realized that Mina wasn't joking, her eyes grew wide. "Dracula-Dracula?"

"Yup."

"The vampire?"

"Yup."

"He's a vampire-vampire, right?"

"Yup. Please stop saying everything twice."

"Okay. You…lost…his cat? Lost-lost?"

"You're doing it again."

"Sorry. What happened?"

Mina gave her the quick and dirty details.

"An *Unspeakable Horror*?"

"Is that what this is?" Rex slid into the table with them, closely examining the slop on his tray. "Has Mina finally gone off the deep-end?"

"She… lost… Dracula's… cat."

"Huh?" Rex was stunned. "You mean Dracula-Dracula?"

"Ungh!" Mina covered her head with her hands. "Please stop-stop! You guys don't understand. I'm losing all of my pet sitting gigs. Everybody from Midnight Villas has called and canceled. I was doing really well and now Zoo Camp will be as impossible as it was before."

"We could help you find the cat. Make nice with the King of Vampires and smooth everything over with the groovie ghoulies."

"Yeah, sounds like a blast," Rex said around a mouthful of spaghetti.

"Really?" Mina sat up in her chair.

"No," Rex said. "Yeah, really. But I can't come. I'm busy.Well thanks," Mina said. "Thanks for nothing."

Rex grinned. "You're welcome for nothing."

"I'll help you. We can figure this out," Vanessa said.

Mina caught Silvia out of the corner of her eye.

"Give me a sec, okay? I need to talk to Silvia."

Rex snorted chocolate milk out of his nose. "Now *I've* gone off the deep end. Did she just say *talk* to Silvia? You don't just communicate with the forces of evil."

"Yeah," Vanessa said. "I think that involves actual human sacrifice."

"Maybe not as human as you might think," Mina muttered, heading for Silvia's table.

"Can I talk to you?"

Silvia looked up at Mina. She was doing her math homework while she ate lunch. When she looked up at Mina, she did not stop writing. Her pen danced across the notebook paper like it was working the problems by itself. "Monster Mina strikes ag…"

"Spare me," Mina said. "I saw you at home last night."

Silvia stopped writing, scowled up at Mina.

"I don't know who you saw or what you think you know, but…"

"Your next-door neighbors are zombies," Mina said.

Silvia's volume dropped. "Are you *threatening* me?"

"No," Mina said. "I'm not, really, but I need your help. I…uh…I lost Dracula's cat."

Silvia flashed a wicked grin. "It isn't my fault that you took a winged cat downtown without a leash. Get away from me, M…" Mina could tell she was going to call her *Monster*, but Silvia stopped just short. "…and, stay out of my neighborhood." Silvia dropped her fork on the table. It was crushed into a steel lump in her bare hand.

Mina knew she should be frightened, but it was her turn to grin wickedly instead. "I never said anything about taking a winged cat downtown."

Silvia's too-blue eyes glared at her.

Mina backed away from the table and returned to her friends. She sat down.

"Uh, why are you smiling?" Vanessa lifted an eyebrow.

"Because I didn't say anything about taking a cat downtown," she said. "But she knew. How would she know? Unless…"

Mr. Smith's science lab was dark when Mina went to the door and she turned and started to walk away when a voice from inside called her back.

Mina stepped inside the room, squinting as her eyes adjusted to the dark. She didn't see anyone. In the dark, the lab seemed very creepy. Jars of unidentifiable creatures lined high shelves. Equipment was tucked in every corner like a yard sale at Dr. Frankenstein's house. "Hello?"

"Up here," Mr. Smith said. He was standing on a ladder and trying to change a long fluorescent light bulb. The bulb didn't seem to want to fit in the light fixture and Mr. Smith dropped the bulb and nearly fell off the ladder trying to catch it, only to snag it at the last second. "How many science teachers does it take to screw in a light bulb?"

Mina smiled. "Uh, I don't know."

Mr. Smith shook his head with disappointment. "Apparently, neither do I." He began to climb down the ladder. Halfway down, he stopped and sneezed, then dug a handkerchief out of his lab coat pocket. "When I was younger I used to tease my grandfather about using a handkerchief, told him he was blowing his nose and keeping it. Now, I see your average tissue can't hold up against my sneezes. Without a handkerchief, I wind up blowing my nose with my hand."

Gross, Mina thought. "Do you have a cold?"

"Allergies, I'm afraid. I've always had them, but enough about my mucus, Mina, what can I do for you today?"

Mina took a deep breath. It was now or never. "It's about Silvia," she said.

Mr. Smith sighed. "You've no idea how many times a day I have a conversation like this. Did she steal your boyfriend, your spot on the team or your immortal soul?"

"Cat. I think she stole my cat. Well, the cat I was pet sitting for."

"A cat. Well, that *is* a new one," he said. "That is a very serious accusation. What makes you think that Silvia kidnapped your cat, that she would even be capable of such action?"

"When I asked her for help, she seemed to know more about it then I thought she should."

"Yes, and?"

Mina didn't know what to say. "We've had…disagreements, I guess you could call them, in the past. We're not the best of friends."

"No, I gathered that much." he said. "I heard that you embarrassed her quite a bit on the basketball court the other day in Physical Education."

"You heard about that?"

"Yes, I did. Is it possible that the particular cat you were pet sitting was just too much for you? I know Silvia isn't the easiest person to get along with, but…"

"It was Dracula's cat. I searched Midnight Villas trying to find him. I saw her there. I know that Silvia is a monster and…I guess…that makes you one, too."

The smile faded from Mr. Smith's face. He removed his thick, black glasses and rubbed his eyes with his fingers. "Is that how it is, then? You've lost Count Dracula's cat and now it is time to find someone to blame? Your arch nemesis, maybe? Make Silvia look…bad. Look worse in front of the school and the community. I suggest you leave. I have a light bulb to change." He turned from her then and climbed back up the ladder, light bulb in hand.

"Do you mind if I ask you one more question?"

"If you must."

"What are you allergic to?"

She could tell that he did not want to say. He held back the truth like someone trying hard not to puke. "Cats," he said. "I'm allergic to cats."

11
SILVIA'S HOUSE

"I HATE TO complain," Vanessa said, pedaling awkwardly alongside Mina that day after school. She seemed to be having a hard time keeping up.

"No you don't," Mina said. "You love to complain. You live to complain. You are the *queen* of complaining."

"Bow before the queen, peasant," Vanessa said. "But seriously, I haven't ridden a bike since I was a little kid and they took the training wheels off." She wobbled again and almost went over. She was pure style and grace on horseback, but on a bike, not so much.

"I really appreciate you helping me with this," Mina said.

"No problem."

They had already searched near the school and downtown and all the places in between; Mina's neighborhood, and Vanessa's. They even checked the animal shelter.

But they didn't find Belfry.

"There's one last place to check," Mina said.

"I was afraid you'd say that," Vanessa said.

The gates of Midnight Villas looked like the gates to a spooky old graveyard with iron bars and dusty old, stone walls. They were nothing compared to the protection spell that guarded the place. The two girls coasted to a stop just outside the gates.

"Creeptacular," Vanessa said.

"Really not that bad," Mina said, "In fact, pretty much like a normal neighborhood."

Vanessa looked sideways at Mina. "My neighborhood doesn't have a crashed spaceship or, ya'know, a pyramid."

Holding hands, they passed through the protective barrier that surrounded Midnight Villas. Both of them shivered.

They pedaled down the street. Vanessa froze in front of the House that Scares Monsters. "Whoa, freaky," she said. "Somebody really should burn that place to the ground."

They stared at the old house. The wind swung a hanging shutter on the second floor. It banged against the outside of the house.

Vanessa held up one hand. "No wind."

"You noticed that, too? My dad said it isn't just haunted that it's…full of fear."

"Full of fear," Vanessa repeated. She shivered. "Let's just get out of here, okay?"

"The kids at school would kill to get this far into Midnight Villas," Mina said.

Vanessa stared warily at the many spooky houses. "Well, the kids at school aren't very bright, are they?"

"Let's just get this over with. Look, there's somebody over there we can talk to." Mina pointed to a man in his front yard of a small castle, clipping hedges with a pair of rusty shears.

"Are you sure he's…alive?"

"Well, he's moving."

"That proves nothing," Vanessa said, hanging back as Mina got closer.

"Hello sir," Mina said and realized who it was. Frankenstein. She recognized him from the movies and TV, although in person, he was even…grosser. Mina could see where he had been assembled from many different people. His arms weren't the same length and neither were his legs, which made him stand a little crooked. He looked at her with two different colored eyes. Mina thought she could see his brain squeezing out a little between the stitches holding the top of his head on. Mina shuddered. Vanessa stepped away and Mina grabbed her by the wrist. "Mr. Frankenstein. I was wondering…"

"Yeah, what?" He clipped the hedge. The blades clanked together.

"My name is Mina and I'm looking for a black cat

with…"

"Wings, yeah, I know. Dracula's cat, Belfry." His voice sounded like his throat was full of dirt and gravel.

He clipped the hedge again, louder this time. Clank!

"Yeah, so you know all about it. Uh, great! Well, I'm trying to find…"

"You lost him." He clipped again, but this time got a tree as big as Mina's waist in his clippers. The tree came off cleanly and fell back into his yard smashing his flowerbed.

Frankenstein looked at the tree and the squashed flowers like they didn't really matter and then at Mina and Vanessa. Without a word, he walked back to his house and went inside.

"I think that went well," Vanessa said, clapping her hands together. "Maybe next time we could talk to someone who could just go ahead and *eat* us."

Rex skated up alongside of them. "I know where the cat is," he said, and turned left down the street.

The girls looked at each other. "How did *you* find him?"

"Wait up, Rex," Vanessa said, struggling to turn her bike around.

Rex said nothing and, after an uncertain second, they followed him.

"I THINK MY butt went to sleep," Vanessa said, shifting uncomfortably behind the hedges in Silvia Smith's yard. They'd been huddled in the landscaping for an hour.

"Well, wake it up." Mina said, peeking over the top of the hedges next to Rex. "So, you saw Belfry here?"

"Not *exactly*," Rex said.

"Well, what then?"

"He's in that house. Trust me."

"Besides, I thought you said you were too busy to help us look," Vanessa said.

"You both have serious trust issues."

"That is Silvia Smith's house," Mina said. "I talked to Mr. Smith already. I asked him if Silvia took Belfry."

"Whoa," Rex said. "*Silvia Smith* lives in Midnight Villas. That means she's…"

"Yup," Mina said. She knew the truth and it still seemed impossible to her. Besides her lousy personality, she seemed so normal. "She's a monster."

"Wow, look at this," Vanessa said, pointing at her face with her finger. "This? This is my surprised face," Vanessa said, eyes bulging and mouth hanging open. "I've known Silvia was an evil brat since the second grade."

"What kind of monster do you think she is?" Rex was closely examining the house.

Mina shrugged. She didn't know.

"What kinds of monsters eat cats?" Rex ducked down

with the two girls, squeezing in between the two of them. Mina felt funny being so close to him and something fluttered in her belly. He smelled really good, too; not at all like she would have expected him to smell. She didn't realize that she was staring at the side of his face until he turned and looked at her. She looked away, blushing.

"Gross," Mina said. "She didn't *eat* Belfry. She kidnapped him."

"Cat-napped," Vanessa said. "*Cat-nap*," she said again, and giggled. "Sounds kinda cute when you say it like that."

"Will you two *focus*," Mina said. "She kidnapped Belfry to get back at me for the basketball thing the other day in gym."

"Which was awesome, by the way," Rex said, holding his hand up for a high five. After a second, he added, "Don't leave me hanging."

When Mina didn't high five him, Vanessa did. "Up high," she said.

Mina shook her head. "You two are impossible. How do we even know that he's in there?"

The smile faded from Rex's face. He looked right in Mina's eyes, until she had to look away. "Trust me," he said.

She nodded. She heard herself say, "Okay." Had she lost her mind?

"Well, what are we going to do?" Vanessa said.

Mina had a plan. "I'm pretty sure Silvia is in cheerleading practice…."

"Because she's so darn *cheery*," Rex added.

"I know, right?" Vanessa said.

"Hello?" Mina poked them both with her index fingers. "Secret mission planning going on here. Silvia is at practice, she won't be home…"

"One of us should go keep an eye on her," Vanessa said. "Just in case."

"Okay," Rex said, "you go."

"You're way faster than me, you should go," Vanessa said, backpedaling.

"Rock, paper, scissors?" Rex held out his palm.

Vanessa shrugged. "One, two, three."

"Ah-ha," Rex said, "Paper covers rock. Better get to pedaling."

"*Paper covers rock* makes no sense at all."

"I think my head is going to explode," Mina said, rubbing her temples with her fingers.

"Okay-okay," Vanessa said, heading off on her bicycle.

Mina checked her phone every two minutes, made sure she hadn't muted the ringer and double-checked that she had reception. It took twenty minutes for Vanessa to ride her bike from Silvia's house in Midnight Villas back to the school.

Mina's phone finally rang and she answered. "She

there?"

"I'm looking at her right now," Vanessa said. "Silvia Smith is in cheerleading practice as we speak."

"Great, keep an eye on her. Holler if she leaves."

"Roger," Vanessa said.

Mina pocketed her cell phone. "I'm going in."

"I'll go with you," Rex said, stashing his skateboard in the bushes.

"No, you have to stay here and keep an eye out. If anyone comes home, text me."

Rex looked at the big, strange house suspiciously. "Are you sure that nobody is home now?"

"No cars in the driveway. No lights in the windows." She shrugged. "I'm ready. I think I can see a way to get in."

"You sure you've never broken into a house before? You're really good at this. Maybe you should be a cat burglar to make money."

"Meow," Mina said and hurried from her hiding space among the bushes up to the side of the house. An entire wall of the house on one side was covered with rusty gears bigger than her. She imagined the inside of that giant clock in England, Big Ben, must look like that. The massive gears turned slowly, interlocking with each other. Mina could see where one of the giant wheels disappeared into the wall of the house. Mina leaned forward and when the gear turned her way, she reached out and grabbed a hold of it. It lifted her off the ground and up she went like a Ferris wheel.

She passed through the hole in the wall and she frantically searched for an opening. She eased herself off the wheel as it went around.

Mina snuck down the hallway of the Smith house, not knowing what to expect. The walls were smooth steel, the floor concrete. Above her head, pipes, wires and conduit snaked across the ceiling, running in all direction. The lights were so bright that it reminded her of an operating room. The thought made her belly queasy. She had to squint against the blinding fluorescent bolts to see and the dazzling lights didn't do anything to calm her. It just meant that when she saw something horrible, it wouldn't be hiding in the shadows. She would see it coming.

And she was sure she would see *something* horrible.

Mina checked her phone. No reception. "Wonderful," she whispered.

She placed her hand flat on the cold metal wall. It hummed, vibrating the bones in her arm like it was alive. But what form of life was it?

She pulled her hand away, unconsciously wiping it on her jeans. She missed the good, old-fashioned doom and gloom of Dracula's castle.

She came to a door—the only one in the upstairs hallway.

The door had no knob, but when Mina leaned closer to look for a handle, she must have tripped some kind of switch, because the door slid open automatically like the automatic door at the supermarket.

She went inside. The room looked more like a mechanic's garage than a teenage girl's room. One wall was covered with electronic parts, mechanical pieces and shiny steel tools, arranged neatly on the wall and on the organized top of a workbench. A laptop computer sat on the desk.

Where a bed would have been was a big steel worktable. Wires and pipes snaked from the top of the table and dangled down from the ceiling.

Mina took out her phone to take a picture. Her phone showed that she wasn't getting any reception inside the house.

She gulped. *Not good.* What if Vanessa was trying to call? Or Rex?

Downstairs she could hear another door slide open. She heard voices.

Mr. Smith, *and Silvia!* How did she get home so fast?

Mina looked around the room. A closet full of clothes took up the whole wall. She slipped into the closet and hid behind a long coat.

Someone came into the room.

Mina peeked out from behind the coat. Of course it was Silvia. It was *her* room.

Silvia dropped her backpack on the floor. She stretched her slender arms above her head and yawned.

She picked up something from the table. It was a drill. She stuck the screwdriver end into her neck and pulled the trigger.

Mina clamped her hand over her mouth. She wanted to scream. Or puke.

But no blood spurted anywhere. And she kept doing it.

Mina's eyes bulged out of their sockets.

Silvia lifted her head off and set it down on the table. The eyes blinked, looking right at her.

Mina ran.

She was down the hallway and bounding down the stairs three at a time. She didn't even try to sneak. She went out the front door like a rocket.

She found her bike in the bushes and was pedaling like a crazy person. She didn't look back, couldn't. She didn't stop until she rolled to a stop in her own driveway.

"Hey," Rex said, skating to a stop near her. Vanessa caught up to them a minute later. He had followed her home from Midnight Villas, calling Vanessa on the way.

"What happened?"

"Silvia Smith," Mina said, "is a robot!"

Rex and Vanessa stood in stunned silence.

"And she came home, but you didn't warn me!"

"I called and called," Vanessa said.

"No reception in the house," Mina said, shaking her head.

"No, I mean, one minute she was there and the next minute she was gone. I swear. I never took my eyes off of her," Vanessa said.

"Did you find the cat?"

"No, Rex, I didn't. He wasn't there. So, as always, thanks for nothing!"

Rex looked at the ground. He turned, got on his skateboard and disappeared into the darkening night.

"That was harsh," Vanessa said. "He was trying to help."

"She took her head off in front of me! Her head! Off!"

"I guess I wasn't much help either, huh?"

"Not really," Mina said, "I mean, you know what I mean."

Vanessa nodded, without making eye contact. "It's getting late. I gotta go." Vanessa climbed onto her bike and pedaled away.

Mina stood alone on the sidewalk, watching her friends leave. She shivered, rubbing her arms with her hands. She realized how dark it was getting and went inside.

That night, Mina sat in her bed staring out the window. With the blankets pulled up to her chin, she waited to see two red, robot eyes staring at her out of the dark.

What was she going to do now?

12
FATHER AND DAUGHTER

THE NEXT DAY, Mina fell asleep in her breakfast, snoozing in her mother's amazing French toast. She wasn't going to make it through the day, and if it wasn't bad enough that she had been up all night waiting for Silvia to come and get her, she also had butterflies the size of vultures in her belly over her static with Vanessa and Rex. She stared out the bathroom window at the grayish morning waiting for her.

And then she missed the bus.

Without so much as a word, her mom frowned when she dropped her off at school. Mina had to dash down the empty hallway to not be tardy for homeroom.

She had wanted to apologize to Vanessa and, to a lesser extent, Rex for her behavior. But she was so tired that she was almost glad to miss them in the morning assembly. Mina sighed. She wished she'd tried to get off today as a sick day. Too late for that now.

It took every bit of energy and concentration that she had for Mina not to fall asleep in homeroom, even though many students did, she didn't want to drool on her desk. Billy Anderson fell asleep in homeroom on a regular basis and he snored *and* drooled. Kids put balls of notebook paper in his mouth while he slept. Once, he almost choked to death on a pink eraser thrown from halfway across the room. Her own social standing could not survive a hit like that.

Between classes, she saw Mr. Smith in the hallway by Silvia's locker. He jerked his thumb towards the science lab classroom and Silvia slumped and headed that way.

Mina raced up the stairs on the opposite end of the hallway and slipped into Mr. Smith's lab ahead of them. The supply closet hung open. Mina hurried inside and pulled the door almost shut behind her.

Mr. Smith entered. She couldn't see him, but she heard his voice. He was not happy. "I've had to deal with a lot of your behavior, Silvia, and it's getting harder and harder to make excuses for you. I didn't raise you this way."

"You didn't raise me at all, *Dad*. You programmed me. You built me. I'm nothing more than another science project to you!"

"Keep your voice down. Have you lost your mind?"

"I don't have a mind. I have a microprocessor."

"Did you steal that girl's cat?"

"No, of course not. She just has it in for me. She was in our house. She saw me doing…diagnostics."

Mr. Smith fell back against one of the lab tables, rattling a rack of test tubes. He took off his glasses and rubbed his eyes with his fist. "She…she would have had no idea what she was seeing."

"My *head* was not attached to my *body* at the time."

Mr. Smith dropped his glasses. They cracked as they hit the floor. "Well, to make matters worse, this is Count Dracula's cat. He doesn't have a sense of humor on a good day. But when it comes to his cat…"

"I'll deal with it. And with her."

"No, *I'll* deal with it. You just keep your nose clean."

Silvia brushed the tip of her nose with the back of her hand. "Do I have something on my nose?"

Mr. Smith sighed. "No, it's just an expression. It means to stay out of trouble."

"Oh."

"Go ahead, you're already late for class."

She huffed from the room.

Mr. Smith gathered up some papers and left.

Mina crept out of the supply closet.

What did Silvia mean that she would *deal with her*? Mina turned to go to class.

Sylvia grabbed her by the neck and lifted her up off her feet. She moved so fast Mina hadn't even seen her come back into the room.

Mina dropped her backpack and used both hands to try to pry her fingers away from her throat. She would have had better luck trying to bend steel in her bare hands. She could feel just by the strength, that Silvia could have easily popped her head off like a dandelion.

Unnatural blue eyes zeroed in on her. Silvia brought her down until they were face to face. "If I see you in my neighborhood again, in my home, I will kill you. You know what I am and what I can do. This is your one and only warning." Her voice didn't sound right. It was hollow and electronic, like an angry fax machine.

She dropped Mina to the floor.

Mina stayed there, holding her neck, until the bell rang and the next class started.

13
RESCUE?

No matter what Silvia the killer robot said, Mina wasn't about to give up looking for Belfry and if that meant going back to Midnight Villas, then that's what she would do. Before that, though, she had one more place to check and what lurked there was a lot scarier than a robotic bully.

Mina stood at the opening of the forest where she had first encountered the Unspeakable Horror. Her hands shook. Even thought it was only late afternoon, the woods were already getting dark and the trees looked as sharp and dangerous as a mouthful of shark's teeth.

She hadn't had the chance to talk to Vanessa about coming with her. She had been pretty harsh about Silvia's house and her friends didn't seem too thrilled to talk to her. Sighing, she silently wished she didn't have to do this by herself.

As if answering that wish, the black dog appeared out

of the edge of the woods. She petted him on top of his head. "Hey, you," she said.

Mina snuck into the woods trying to be as quiet as possible. She listened, hoping to hear Belfry. The possibility still existed that what she found might not be what she hoped to find. She remembered the small skeletons that she had seen along the path the first time she came through here. She crossed her fingers on both hands, hoping that Belfry hadn't become a snack for the Unspeakable Horror.

She heard running water. A river? She didn't think that there were any close enough to hear. Besides, it seemed to be coming from her left in the woods. She looked at the black dog who was looking back at her. He didn't seem to know his way around these woods any more than she did.

She heard something crying. The black dog's ears went up. He had heard it, too. "C'mon," she said. They ran into the woods, headed for the sound of the water and the crying.

When the noise was at its loudest, Mina stopped and looked around. Nothing. The black dog looked around, too. They looked at each other and then down.

A sewer grate lay beneath them almost completely covered with leaves and branches. The two of them dug through the underbrush until the grate was uncovered. The crying got louder, but it sounded feline. It must be a cat.

"Belfry?" Mina's voice echoed over the sound of running water.

The cry came back to her.

She pulled on the grate, but it didn't budge. She could see that the water level was rising. The sewer must be overflowing.

She looked around and spotted another grate some distance away. She ran for it, the black dog right behind her. She found another, then another until the woods opened up around a wide, deep pit. She climbed down the rocky face to the water until she found the open drainpipe. She yelled into it. It echoed. Mina listened and the cry seemed faint and distant.

"Okay," she said, squatting down and crawling into the end of the pipe. The water was ice cold and it was only a minute before her knees and hands were numb.

The pipe she was crawling in led deep underground until it opened up into a large chamber where several other pipes led away. Sunlight trickled down from above and, as Mina got to her feet, she could tell she was under one of the sewer grates she had run past.

The black dog barked down at her.

"Oh," she said, "there you are. I thought dogs liked to play in the water."

The dog did not reply.

The water level was rising and she noticed that two of the pipes that emptied into the room were already gone under and a third one was half-covered by gross, dirty sewage.

From that pipe, the cry came again. It sounded more frantic and terrified now.

"I can't believe this…" she said and climbed to the pipe. The water was almost covering it. She listened, trying to filter out the endless gurgle of the water.

The cat cried again. There was no way she was going to let Dracula's cat drown…

Mina took several deep breaths and then dunked her head into the water and pushed herself into the pipe. She kicked with her feet and clawed with her hands on the inside of the pipe pulling herself along and thinking about swim camp a summer ago.

She came out the other side of the pipe into another large chamber. She broke the surface and took a deep breath. Above her head, she heard the cat. "Belfry?" She wiped the mucky water out of her eyes.

It wasn't Belfry.

Mina's shoulders slumped. Her stomach bottomed out. The creature was about as big as a teddy bear and its eyes blinked at her. She blinked back. She could not believe what she was seeing.

It was a *baby* Unspeakable Horror.

Its fur was matted with sewage. He was stuck up on a large pipe, just above the water level. Any minute, the room would be filled with water and both of them would go under. "I hope you can hold your breath, Cutey," Mina said, seizing the creature by the paw.

She took a deep breath and, dragging the creature behind her with one hand, fought her way back down the pipe. This time the water was flowing the same way she was, so it pushed her along faster. When she got back to the sewer grate chamber, all the other pipes were under water. She pulled them both up to the grate to catch a breath. She was so tired her lungs burned and her arms felt limp and loose like overcooked spaghetti.

She wondered where the black dog had gone.

Something licked her hand.

She smiled up through the grate. The black dog was there.

Mina fought to keep herself and the Unspeakable toddler above water, but she was so tired. She felt blackness creeping in around the edge of her eyes. The water was so cold.

She had to stay up, keep on treading water. She had to. She couldn't give up. Not now. Not...

Mina went under.

She thought she felt hands, human hands, grabbing for hers and pulling on the grate.

She wondered who it could be trying to save her—there had been no one there but her and the black dog.

She sank down, staring upward through the bars of the grate. The sky, where she could make it out through the twisted black branches, was dimming.

The grate was suddenly ripped free and she was yanked out of the water, strong hands grabbing the back of her shirt. She collapsed onto the ground, coughing and sputtering as the black dog licked her face happily. "Thank you so much," she said, trying to get up. She was woozy and struggled to stand up. She made it halfway up and fell to her knees. She looked to see who saved her.

The Unspeakable Horror loomed above her. It glared at her. Mina backed away from it. It roared in Mina's face.

The black dog got between Mina and the Horror.

"Here," Mina said, reaching for the young creature. It was dripping wet, but it seemed okay.

The monster mother scooped the creature up in its massive arms and with a final look in Mina's direction, stomped off into the woods.

Mina lay back down on the grass to catch her breath. The black dog curled up in the grass near her. She patted his head.

14
CLOWNS

"You look like a drowned cat," Vanessa said when she answered the door. Mina had pedaled all of the way to the horse ranch.

"You should see the other guy," Mina said. "Can I borrow a towel?"

"How about a shower with that towel?" Vanessa had her very own bathroom in her room. She pushed Mina into the bathroom as she turned on the shower. "You smell like a sewer. What happened?"

Mina shrugged weakly. She really didn't want to talk about it. "I think there are tadpoles in my pocket." She got under the hot water it felt good on her shoulders, but she couldn't take it on her face. It felt like drowning all over again. She sputtered and coughed.

"Is it that bad?"

"Yes. No. Maybe. I don't know."

"What did you do, pet sit for the Loch Ness Monster?"

Mina poked her head out from behind the shower curtain. "No. Why? Is he looking for someone?"

"You're nuts. You know that right?"

"I've had my suspicions for a little while." She quickly washed her hair, twigs and leaves falling to her feet in the shower drain.

"I feel like I don't know you anymore. First, Circus camp. You got into a fistfight with a clown. A clown. You never even told me about that. What, did he do, abuse a balloon animal?"

"No." Mina turned the water off.

"Well, what then?" Vanessa handed her a plush purple towel.

Mina toweled off and then wrapped it around her. "An elephant." She took another towel and wrapped it around her head. "This clown was trying to get it to do this trick where it pretends to step on his foot and he jumps around like he's hurt, but it actually stepped on his foot for real. This clown just went crazy. Started screaming and hitting this elephant with the trainer's whip."

"That really sucks."

"Yeah."

"So, what did you do?"

"I couldn't just stand there…"

"Mina? What did you do?"

"Remember karate camp?"

"Uh, yeah."

"I knocked his…red nose off."

"Not good."

"With my foot."

"Really not good. Did he, I don't know, press charges or whatever?"

"No, probably too embarrassed that he got his, ya'know, nose knocked off by a girl."

"Clown pride?"

"Guess so."

Vanessa handed Mina her hair-dryer. "I'll find you something to wear, okay?"

"Thanks," Mina said and hugged her.

While Mina dried her hair, she looked around Vanessa's gigantic room. A covered bed fit for a princess took up most of the space along with several dressers and a desk. It seemed like it had been a long time since she had been here last.

If there was one thing you couldn't miss in Vanessa's room was her love of horses. Her walls were lined with posters and pictures of horses. There were photographs of Vanessa competing in horse riding events. In one, she was jumping an obstacle on the back of her horse, Odyssey. The look on her face was pure determination. Blue ribbons hung everywhere in the room. It didn't seem like she ever lost when a horse was involved.

From her bedroom window, Mina could see the stables. A trainer was walking a small horse in a great big circle.

Vanessa emerged from her enormous closet carrying a skirt and a top. The skirt was zebra striped. Vanessa looked very proud of herself. Her smile was infectious. Mina felt sad and happy at the same time. "What do you think?"

Mina smiled. "Perfect." She looked at the floor. "I went looking for Belfry." Mina told her what happened. About the Unspeakable Horror and the sewer.

Vanessa hugged her, but said nothing.

15
SCARY HOUSES

THE NEXT DAY at lunch, Mina told Rex about the previous day's adventure. Rex seemed not too interested, but Vanessa still shook her head.

"You could have drowned or been eaten or drowned and then been eaten."

"It isn't as bad as it sounds." She tried to play it off, but she had been terrified when the water went over her head. Now, she didn't even like the idea of taking a bubble bath, which had been one of her favorite things to do.

"Sounds like you almost drowned," Rex said. It almost seemed like he was reading her mind.

Mina shrugged.

"I don't see why you don't just quit with this cat," Rex said. "I mean, you aren't even getting paid for this and you keep sticking your neck out for this guy's cat. He told you to mind your own business, didn't he?"

"I don't expect you to understand," Mina said. Rex was

right, she thought. Why was she still messing with this? It wasn't about the Zoo Camp anymore. Now, she was really worried for Belfry. She didn't know what happened to him and she was really worried that he was hurt and needed help. It had been her job to take care of the poor cat and now he was missing and Count Dracula had been heartbroken over it, if vampires could even be heartbroken. It certainly sounded like it when she heard him crying.

Silvia walked by, glaring at Mina.

Mina smiled back at her.

Vanessa and Rex tried not to look, but couldn't help it.

The three of them sat in total silence. "Think she has *Wi-Fi*?"

They burst out laughing.

That gave Mina an idea. "You think you could distract her for a minute?"

Rex grinned. "Distraction is my specialty. What do you have in mind?"

Mina leaned over and whispered her plan to the other two.

"Me likey," Rex said, picking up his skateboard. "Maybe this will finally get me expelled," he said hopefully.

Silvia was doing homework on her computer and eating lunch simultaneously, although Mina noticed for the first time that she never actually ate anything, she just moved the food around her tray and then threw it away.

"For my next trick..." Rex said, suddenly jumping his skateboard from the floor up to the edge of the table Silvia was sitting at and sliding along the edge. He hit her milk and dumped it in her lap. Rex laughed. "A rail ride with a splash!" Silvia jumped up like the Wicked Witch of the West getting doused with water. Mina wondered absently if she would short circuit. Not exactly her plan, but it would have been a happy coincidence.

While Silvia was getting napkins to mop up the milk, Mina grabbed her laptop computer and quickly checked her internet search history. She saw a website that said *home for sale*. She quickly clicked on that.

The House that Scares Monsters popped up. Mina's mouth hung open.

Silvia grabbed the computer out of her hands.

"Just trying to keep that from getting wet for you. You know how wonky electronic junk can get."

Silvia growled at her. Mina grinned.

Rex and Mina returned to the seat with Vanessa as Silvia stormed out of the cafeteria. "Well, what did you find out?"

Mina couldn't believe she had not thought of that before. "I learned that robots aren't afraid of ghosts." Silvia had been checking on the House that Scares Monsters, maybe even going there, and maybe even stashing a kidnapped cat there.

Thanks to Silvia's laptop, Mina thought she knew where Belfry was being hidden. Unfortunately, that meant Mina would have to go inside the House that Scares Monsters.

16
SUPERCREEPOPEDIA

Mina often had dreams of flying, but this was the first one where she had actual wings to do it, big bat-like wings that stretched farther than her arms and grew from the tips of her fingers: huge, leathery wings, just like Belfry's.

She flew through the streets of Midnight Villas, soaring past castles and haunted houses at dizzying speeds.

The sky was gray and cloudy and the air was cold. She shivered against an icy wind that blew right through her.

But Mina was afraid; she didn't like to fly.

"What have you done?" She knew the voice. It cracked on the edge of tears. Count Dracula! He ran along the ground beneath her, clawing at her with his hands. "I trusted you!" His long black coat flew behind him as he ran.

"Monster Mina strikes again," Silvia said, although now she was a metal skeleton wired together with claws and fangs and her perfect blond hair. She chased her, too, leaping on her mechanical legs, nearly grabbing her with her steel talons.

Mina flapped her bat-wings faster, but now she wasn't just like Belfry...she *was* Belfry.

Mina knew Silvia was getting closer.

She felt Silvia's robotic claws close on her tail and she was suddenly yanked out of the sky. She hung by her tail in front of Silvia's face. An Unspeakable Silvia! *So not good!*

She unhinged her jaw like a python and swallowed cat-Mina whole.

Mina screamed!

Mina woke clawing at the sweaty tangle of blankets on her bed. Gasping for air, she didn't even know where she was for a moment. Slowly, her head cleared.

Now more than ever, she had to find Belfry. It was the only way to help Dracula. It was also the only way she would ever get back her other pet sitting gigs and earn enough money to go to Zoo Camp, and that meant she had to prove to Mr. Smith and everyone that Silvia had catnapped Belfry.

She looked at her *Animals are People, too* poster.

She sighed. What was she thinking? The only thing that mattered now was finding Belfry and getting him back home.

Animals she knew. Monsters? Not so much. Besides

Count Dracula, she didn't know much about monsters at all.

That was it—where did she go to learn everything that was actually interesting? Certainly not school. The really good stuff…

She hopped out of bed and opened her laptop computer. She went straight to *supercreepopedia.com*. She searched *robots*.

Under *robots*, she clicked on *weaknesses*:

Unlike vampires (crosses, holy water, garlic) and werewolves (wolfsbane and silver bullets), robots do not have a supernatural weakness. As they are man-made and not actually magical, very little seems to hurt them. They are difficult to identify as they can be made in any shape or form. Although they are machines, many of them have near-human emotions and can be angered.

"No kidding," Mina said. Beneath the text, there was a photo of a metal skeleton with razor-sharp fangs and wires dangling from it. Its hand ended in powerful claws. Mina rubbed her throat where Silvia had grabbed her. Mina stared at the picture and wondered if that's what Silvia looked like underneath her blond hair and too-blue eyes.

She scratched her head. What else? Black dog! Mina went back to the search bar and typed in *black dog*. "Probably nothing, but…" A picture of a monstrous black beast popped up. "Uh-oh."

> *Black dogs are often ghosts or demons in Britain or Ireland and often are considered bad luck or as portents of doom, often appearing before the death of someone nearby.*

"Doom," she whispered. The black dog wasn't a ghost, was he? He had saved her life a couple of times. Not every black dog in the world was some kind of monster.

She turned her computer off and glanced out the window. It was dark and late. "Time to go to work," Mina said.

17
ATTACKED!

THE HOUSE THAT Scares Monsters was pretty creepy from a distance, but up close, well, Mina thought it was *much creepier*.

It really was looking at her. She could feel it. The broken out windows on the second floor glared at her. Mina couldn't help think of the front door as an enormous mouth ready to swallow her whole. She couldn't believe she was actually going in there.

She hid her bicycle at the edge of the forest and crept up the creaky steps to the front porch. She wished that Vanessa and Rex were there, but this was something she had to do on her own. She couldn't put her friends in danger.

The front door was boarded shut with dusty old boards and rusty nails. It looked like no one had been there in a while.

Mina shook her head uncertainly. She was sure Belfry

was here. The only problem was she didn't know what else lurked in the most haunted house in the monster neighborhood... But it didn't matter—if Belfry was in there, and she was pretty sure he was, she was going to rescue him and take him back to Dracula where he belonged.

She looked around, wishing that at least the black dog was there. Portent of doom or not, it would have been nice to have some company.

Mina tried a few of the boards, but they were nailed on tight. She checked the windows, but they were even tighter than the doors. She crept around the wraparound porch until she found herself back at the front door. For a deserted, old spook house, it was locked down pretty well.

There was a small metal door just above the ground. It was only big enough that she could climb into it on her hands and knees. *COAL* it said in raised iron letters.

Coal chute, she thought. Houses used to burn coal for heat and they got it delivered through a chute that went from outside into the basement.

Mina slid her fingers beneath the metal door and, with all her strength, forced it open. The rusty hinge screamed. When it was all the way open, Mina stared down the dark, dusty throat of the coal chute. "No spiders, no spiders, no spiders," she repeated as she inched into the opening.

The slightest sound echoed up from the depths of the basement.

Mina strained to listen.

"*Me-ow.*"

"Belfry?" Mina leaned forward into the chute, straining to listen. It could be nothing. It could be another cat. "It could be a ghost," Mina said out loud and immediately wished she hadn't. She leaned forward a bit more and fell face first into the darkness.

Mina tumbled down the chute like Alice going down the rabbit hole. Landing on her face on the basement floor, she wondered if Alice had hit quite so hard.

She dug in her backpack and produced her flashlight. She flipped the switch, but nothing happened. Broken.

"Wonderful."

She dug her phone out of her pocket and flipped it open. The gray light illuminated the basement just beyond her arm's reach. Shadows danced and leaped all around her. She found herself sitting on top of a pile of dusty coal in a large metal bin.

Shadows like tentacles moved in the glow and she yelped.

In the light, the boiler looked like a big hungry mouth, its gauges like eyes that stared at her.

But it was all just a trick of the light.

If there had been a metal monster waiting for her, it would be Silvia Smith. No sign of her, though.

"*Meow.*" The sound seemed to be coming out of the

ice-cold furnace, but when Mina flipped the grate open, she realized that the sound could be coming from any room in the house as the pipes and heating ducts ran all over the place.

"*Meow.*"

Mina sighed. She climbed down out of the coal bin and crept across the basement floor to an iffy looking set of wooden stairs that led upwards. She scrambled up, hoping nothing would grab her ankles through the openings.

The first floor was sparsely decorated with sheet-covered furniture, giving the impression of a wild party of misshapen ghosts. "Stop thinking about ghosts," she said in a low voice. She was actually surprised. Her biggest fears were snakes and spiders and so far she hadn't even seen a spider-web. Maybe, the fear had the night off. Or maybe the phantom snakes ate the ghost's spiders. Mina almost laughed at the thought.

Somewhere in the dark, she heard water drip.

She turned in a quick circle. The light on her phone went out.

Something moved. Mina could hear wet footsteps on the dusty floor. She shut her phone and opened it back up. The dim light revealed wet footprints that passed right next to her. She backed up.

Mina did a quick search of the first floor, found nothing and immediately mounted the stairs to go up to the second floor. Halfway up the stairs, she saw water dripping from the ceiling.

She stopped in her tracks.

The ceiling above her was covered with wet footprints.

"I would rather find snakes." Mina kept going up, trying hard not to look at the ceiling.

The second floor of the house was a maze of rooms and collapsed walls. Moldy doors hung from their hinges. Water dripped from a stain on the ceiling to a puddle on the rug.

In another room, Mina heard someone step. The sound squished. She did not want to see what was making that sound.

"*Meow*," she heard.

"Belfry!" Mina ran up the stairs to the top floor hallway.

"*Meow*."

She burst through the doors into the master bedroom. But there was no Belfry.

Only Silvia! She stood in the middle of the room. She didn't look surprised to see Mina. Silvia smiled. Mina wished she didn't. "*Meow*," Silvia said in a perfect simulation of Belfry.

Mina stumbled backwards, spun around and ran.

Silvia was behind her. "*Meow!*"

Mina swiveled her head and saw Silvia gaining on her.

But then another Silvia stepped out of the darkness. "*Meow.*"

Mina froze. Robots. There was more than one of them. That was how she managed to be in more than one place at a time. "Your dad must really like you," Mina said. "I guess somebody has to."

"He's not my father, monster, he's my creator. And yeah, he's very proud of his creation. *Me.*"

"No wonder you get so much homework done."

"Dracula is on his way here right now. I called him," Silvia said.

"Why would you steal his cat and then call him? That doesn't make any sense. You might have a computer virus in your hard drive."

"I didn't steal his cat. You did, and you kept it here. I was just lucky enough to hear it calling for help and come to the rescue."

"You evil little *toaster.*"

"I don't know what Dracula will do to you when he finds you here with his cat. Especially, when he seems what shape it's in." She dumped a cloth bag on the floor with a thump.

"Belfry!"

"Don't worry, it's just sleeping—for now."

Mina felt anger heating up inside of her. "If you hurt that cat, I will recycle you with my bare hands."

"You're pretty mouthy considering its three against one and, oh yeah, I come from a family of robotic killing machines. I've upgraded."

She has a point, Mina thought, looking at the three robots. They looked identical, but...

"So, which one of you guys is the *original*...Sylvia 1.0?"

"I am," the three of them said in unison.

"Actually," one of the Silvias said. "*I* am the original model."

"Well, then," Mina said. "I guess one of you guys is the improved version, right? Some of the bugs worked out. Maybe a little prettier?"

"No," Silvia 1.0 said.

"Yes," Silvia 2.0 said. "Father upgraded both our processor speed and our beauty subroutines."

"Then," Silvia 3.0 said. "I must be perfection."

"Shut up," Silvia 1.0 said, grabbing both of them by the arms and giving them a shake.

"Release me, prototype," one of the Silvias said, but Mina had lost track of which was which.

Mina grabbed the bag with the cat in it.

A metal hand clamped on her arm.

One of the Sylvia's blue eyes glowed a hateful red.

"Ouch," Mina said.

A black flash rocketed from the darkness and struck Silvia, knocking her down. Mina yanked her arm free.

The black dog!

It backed the Silvia-bot up. It barked like it was going to bite her face off.

"Good dog," Mina said, opening the bag to get Belfry.

Another Silvia grabbed the bag and, with inhuman strength, yanked it out of Mina's hands.

"Let it go. This is over!" Mina grabbed for the bag.

"No, I always win," Silvia said and tossed the bag out the window.

Mina jumped out after it.

The bag tumbled down a story and got caught in the branches of the spooky tree. Belfry was caught in the bag and the branches and could not free himself to fly. If he fell, he would die.

Mina caught a branch. "Circus camp," she said, swinging down from one branch to another.

The bag shifted in the branches, ready to fall.

Mina landed on the branch above it, knocking the wind out of her.

Belfry fell.

Mina jumped, catching the bag and holding tight…

She shook the bag open so that Belfry could escape and he poked his head out. Then Mina fell.

Belfry's wings unfolded and he soared into the night air.

Mina smiled as she fell, but she knew the ground was

going to hurt.

Belfry caught the collar of her coat between his teeth and the two of them fell together.

Mina and Belfry glided toward the ground together. It was still too fast, but she thought it might be okay, it was…

They hit the ground like a rock.

Mina looked up and Dracula stood over her.

"Am I alive?" Mina smiled. "Here's your cat, Mr. D. Here's Belfry."

"Miss Mina," Dracula said. "I think your arm…it is hurt."

"Yeah" Mina said, grimacing.

A dog barked and Mina looked up. The black dog gave her one look before disappearing into the woods. "Good dog," she said.

"I'll call your parents," Dracula said, producing a black cell phone from his long coat.

"I'm dead now," Mina said, resting her head on the grass. "Sooo dead."

18
BUSTED

MINA SAT ON the couch in the living room, her arm in a purple splint. A couple of weeks and it would be fine. Her mother stood in front of her, hands on her hips, shaking her head. Her father paced the room. The angrier they got, the faster her mother shook her head and the faster her father paced. They were both going full throttle now.

"You lied to us," her father said. "I told you not to hang up your fliers in the monster neighborhood and you did it anyway."

"I never actually lied to you," Mina said. "Technically. I just left out a few…details."

"Details?" Her mother stopped shaking her head. Bad sign. "You call Count Dracula, the king of the vampires, a *detail*? You call losing his cat a *detail*? How about breaking into a haunted house in Midnight Villas? Is that a detail, too? How about falling out a window?"

"I didn't fall."

Somebody knocked on the front door. Mina's dad went to answer it. "This isn't over, yet," he said. He opened the door.

Count Dracula stood in the darkness on the front porch, a *get well soon* balloon clutched in his pale hand. "Good evening," he said.

"Count," Mina's dad sputtered.

"I wanted to thank your daughter for rescuing my cat and make sure she was not injured too gravely."

"She's in here," her father said, turning toward the living room.

Dracula cleared his throat. Vampires had to be invited into your home before they could enter.

"Oh, I'm sorry, please come in."

"I thank you," the vampire said, stepping across the threshold. He saw Mina sitting on the couch and her mother standing over her with her hands on her hips angrily. "I hope I am not interrupting."

"Oh, no," Mina said. "They were just telling me why I shouldn't pet sit for monsters."

Mina's parents looked at their feet.

"Well," he said. "They are your parents and I'm sure they are just trying to protect you. I am sure if they saw you leap out that window to save Belfry…"

"You *jumped* out of the window?!" Mina's mother

looked like she was going to explode.

"You don't understand! An evil robot threw him out the window. I had to save him!"

"There was an evil robot involved?"

"Three, actually," Mina said, hiding her face with her hands. She was digging her own grave here.

"That was actually the other reason I stopped by," Dracula said, remembering the balloon. He handed it to her. "If you tie it around your wrist, you won't lose it."

"Thanks," she said and quickly knotted it on her arm.

"I would like to know the identity of the robot or robots involved. So that I may destroy them."

Mina swallowed hard. This was the part she had been dreading. She didn't like Silvia, but if she told Dracula who it was, she was going to wind up dead or deactivated or out of order or whatever happened to robots when they were...*destroyed*. She didn't think it was her place to do that. "I don't know who it was. Just some, ya'know, evil robots."

Dracula squinted at her. "I...trust you, Ms. Mina. You are the smartest, bravest and most honorable young woman I have met in many centuries. And from this moment on, you are under the protection of Count Vlad Dracula, King of the Vampires."

Her parents' anger seemed to cool. Her mother forced a smile. "That is really nice of you to say."

"Oh, and I've spoken to several of my creature colleagues and they are interested in your pet sitting services, if you haven't given up the business. Even Frankenstein."

Mina looked at her parents.

Grimacing, they nodded that it was okay.

Belfry poked his head out of Dracula's coat.

Mina's father sneezed suddenly.

Startled, Belfry hissed and sprang from Dracula's coat and flew out the open door.

Dracula sighed. "He's always doing that." He looked at Mina. "I could really use some help, Ms. Mina."

"I'm ready when you are, Count," she said, following him out the door. "I mean, as long as it's okay with my mom and dad."

"I guess a pet sitter has to do what a pet sitter has to do," her mother said. "You better go get that cat."

19
BAD DOG

"SO, YOUR PARENTS are going to let you keep pet sitting?" Vanessa caught Mina in the hall the next day at school.

"Yep, looks like Dracula convinced them," Mina said, taking her science book out of her locker. If she was going to be a veterinarian, she had to work harder at science.

"I knew it was all going to work out," Rex said, tossing his books into his locker across the hall.

"You? You were the one who said I should just give up!"

"I was just kidding," he said, taking off his black hoodie. He never took off that hoodie, but the air-conditioning was out that day and the hallways were scorching. He turned back to her.

"Why would you joke about something like that?"

"I have my reasons," he said. Mina's eyes went to his neck. He was wearing a fancy red dog caller. "You don't know everything that there is to know about me, *Mina*." He headed off to class.

Grinning, Mina watched him go. He was the black dog. Somehow. That's how he got into Midnight Villas. That's how he knew Belfry had been in the House that Scares Monsters. Why did he help her? She grinned to herself.

"Bad dog," she said. Her phone rang and she answered, "Hello, this is Mina, Paranormal Pet Sitter. How can I help you?"

THE END

An excerpt from Monster Pets 2:

THE ALIEN'S SLIME!

"So, what do you think Zoo Camp is going to be like?" Mina said, flipping through the pages of a wildlife magazine. She was sprawled on the floor of her bedroom, her best friend Vanessa nearby on the zebra-striped beanbag chair.

"Okay, I guess," Vanessa said, not looking up from her horse magazine.

"Okay? Okay?" Mina said. "A summer spent working in an actual zoo? What could be cooler than that?"

Vanessa shrugged, lazily flipping pages. "It'll be…alright. I guess."

Mina huffed. "Are you just saying that so I won't be devastated when I can't go?"

Vanessa fought a smile. "Maybe. Okay, it will be awesome, are you happy now? Besides, you're parents said you could go."

"If," Mina said, "If I can earn enough money with this

whole paranormal pet sitting thing and that's a big if. Since things went sideways with Count Dracula's cat, things have been pretty lean."

"I have a good feeling about this," Vanessa said. "Let's just talk about something else, okay?

The two girls sat in silence for a moment before Vanessa joked, "So, uh, you going to do the science fair this year?"

They both laughed. Nobody bothered with the science fair because Silvia Smith won every year. Every year. She was the daughter of the science teacher, Mr. Smith and if that wasn't enough to ensure her continued victories, she was also a robot—a nasty android in a cheerleader uniform. "Yeah, let me get right on that," Mina said, "Why don't you do it?"

"Nah," Vanessa said. "I'm not really science-girl. Besides, you want to be a veterinarian some day, right? Gonna need science for that."

Mina frowned. Vanessa was right, she did want to become a veterinarian and science was important. "What would I even do for a project?"

"How about an aerodynamic study of cats with wings?" Vanessa burst out laughing.

Mina threw a pillow at her. "How about how crazy horse people are?"

Vanessa stopped laughing. "The truth stings, I'll admit

it." She smiled, "But really, you should think about entering."

"Maybe I will."

"You should."

"Oh, I will."

"You should…whoa!"

Mina's cell phone jumped out of her hand and floated up to the ceiling, wrapped in a green glow. The girl's watched it, eyes wide.

Vanessa pointed at it with one shaking finger. "Uh…new app?"

Mina flashed Vanessa a look. "Not exactly."

The light spread out from the cell phone, projecting an image on the wall above their heads. Mina saw stars and planets, but she didn't recognize any of them.

"I hope you have unlimited intergalactic minutes on your phone…"

"What do you mean?"

"That's outside the Milky Way galaxy."

"Wait, I thought you weren't science-girl?"

Vanessa shrugged. "I have my moments."

"Look," Mina said, pointing at the green glow. "It's moving!" It was moving. Flashing through space at warp speed. "There's our solar system, Earth, The United States, Archer's Landing…" Mina already knew where it was headed.

Midnight Villas—the monster neighborhood. She thought she recognized the green glow.

The UFO in Midnight Villas appeared, projected against the wall.

"I... I understand," Mina said out loud. "I'll be there tomorrow after school." The glow quit suddenly and Mina's phone fell. She caught it, smiling. She had another pet sitting gig. "You want to meet some aliens?"

Vanessa shrugged. "Sure, I could go for a close encounter."

Sometime after midnight that night, Mina woke up thirsty, the inside of her mouth feeling like a wool sock. Rubbing her eyes, she staggered down the hallway toward the kitchen. She noticed that the light was on in her dad's office.

"Hey," she said, shielding her eyes from the light.

"What are you doing up, pumpkin?"

"Thirsty. You?"

"Frankestein's tax returns. He's made up of the parts of, like, five different dead bodies. I have to file a different tax return for each body."

"Nasty." Mina said and yawned. Mina's dad was a very special kind of accountant: an accountant for actual monsters. Dracula, Frankenstein and the Mummy, just to name a few. Sometimes it was cool and interesting, but most of the time it was just boring and gross. Mostly gross.

"And, on top of that…"

Mina held her throat with her hand like she was choking and croaked, "Thirsty."

"Okay, honey, good night."

Mina trudged the rest of the way down the hallway to the kitchen, drew a big, cold glass of water from the sink and stood guzzling it down. Mina stared out the window into the night. A loan light post stood on the opposite side of the street and, Mina noticed, that a man stood beneath it.

Mina squinted at him. He wore a black suit and for a moment Mina thought it was her friend, Count Dracula. But, it wasn't.

"Mina?"

Mina jumped dropping her glass. It shattered on the floor.

"I'm sorry," Mina's dad said. "Didn't mean to scare you."

"No," she said, "there's a guy out there." But, when Mina looked the man was gone.

Mina's dad looked out the window, pulling the curtains aside. "It isn't Dracula is it?"

"No, I…I don't think so," Mina looked out the window again. Nobody.

"This paranormal pet sitter business…it isn't dangerous, right?"

"Nope," Mina said. "Just hamsters and stuff."

"It's the *and stuff* that I'm worried about."

Mina yawned and stretched dramatically. "Tonight is a school night…"

"Yeah," he said, looking at her one final time. "I'll clean this up, you better get back to bed."

She yawned again for real. As she turned to go, she snuck one last look out the window, but nobody was there.

Funny.

2
CLOSE CALL IN THE HALL

"FUNNY HA-HA?" Vanessa said, the next day at school. "Or, funny weird?"

"A creepy guy standing outside my window in the middle of the night? Definitely funny weird."

Rex slid into the bleachers next to them. "Funny weird? That would make a great name for a band."

Vanessa shook her head in disbelief. "You say that about everything!"

"No I don't."

Vanessa slid into her dumb boy voice. "Duuude, that would make an *awesome* name for a band!"

"Dude," Rex said, "I don't sound like that. Did you get kicked in the head by a horse again, Nessie?"

"You totally sound like that," Vanessa said. "Doesn't he, Mina?"

"Yeah, what do you think?" Mina shrugged, not looking at Rex.

Vanessa nudged her "C'mon Mina! Back me up here…" But Mina just couldn't look at Rex without blushing. Vanessa rolled her eyes and continued, "Anyway, we're going out to Midnight Villas after school to meet the Aliens. You in?"

Rex jumped up as the morning bell rang. "I'm busy." He bounded down the bleachers and disappeared into the crowd of kids.

Mina and Vanessa watched him go, as they gathered up their backpacks. "Sooo," Vanessa said, "You still think he's a dog?"

Mina nodded her head as they headed down the hall. "Yup." The black dog had saved her many times when she was pet sitting Dracula's cat. It always wore a fancy red dog collar and then she saw the exact same collar on Rex's neck. Coincidence? Mina didn't think so. "It would explain how he got into the protective force-field spell around Midnight Villas and why he's never around when the black dog is."

"I guess everybody has secret, huh?" Vanessa unlocked her locker.

"Yeah, considering what Silvia is…whoa!"

Silvia was suddenly in front of them, staring hard at Mina, a faint red light glowing in the back of her eyes. "What am I, *Monster*?"

Mina cringed away from Silvia's robotic gaze. "Answered your own question there, bright eyes."

Vanessa moved to Mina's side, giving her best tough-cowgirl squint, but Silvia kept her inhuman stare focused on Mina. "Why didn't you rat me out to Dracula?"

"I didn't think…"

"That doesn't make us friends or anything, *Monster*."

"Of course not. Never even occurred to me."

Rex leaned in against the locker next to them. "Hey, Silvia, your Dad was just looking for you. Something about charging your batteries?"

Silvia did turn then, but not without a final warning.

"You better stay out of my way *Monster Mina*."

Mina fell back against the locker and watched Silvia storm away.

"Thanks," Mina said to Rex.

"Ain't no thing," Rex said, smiling, and headed off to class.

Vanessa picked up the backpack that Mina had dropped.

Breathing hard, Mina clenched her fists. After a minute, she marched over to the Science Fair sign-up sheet and scribbled her name under Silvia's.

Vanessa watched the whole thing. "Uh, that doesn't really look like staying out of her way."

Mina grinned. "No, it doesn't, does it?"

3
PLEASED TO SQUEEZE YOU

After the last bell of the day, Mina and Vanessa rode the bus out to Midnight Villas. Mina wanted to ride her bike, but Vanessa couldn't face another bicycle ride. "I've been walking like a cowgirl since last week."

"You *are* a cowgirl," Mina said, staring out the window. She was tapping the glass frantically.

Vanessa grabbed her hand. "You. Must. Chill."

"Sorry. I'm excited, I guess. Maybe nervous."

"Ya think? By the way, do you know if these aliens are the kind that make your bicycle fly or the kind that suck your brains out?"

"Forgot to ask."

"Ask? *Ask?* Oh naïve one, the brain-suckers don't *tell* you that they're brain-suckers, they just, ya'know, suck out your brains."

"That would be embarrassing."

"At very least," Vanessa said.

The old bus rumbled to a stop outside the gates of Midnight Villas. The girls hopped off and stopped just short of a protective force field that kept non-monsters out.

"Ready?"

"Uh..."

Mina grabbed Vanessa's hand and stepped forward, both of them shivering as they passed through the magical field cast by the Voodoo Queen.

Mina had been granted special permission from the king of monsters himself, Count Dracula. She could enter Monster Villas whenever she needed to and as long as she held Vanessa's hand they could walk through together.

Vanessa scowled, as they headed up the sidewalk past Frankenstein's castle. Above their heads sparks of electricity jumped from electrodes that poked high into the sky.

"What?"

"Just wondering."

"What?"

"Well, you have to hold my hand or I can't pass through the force field..."

"Yeah, so?"

"What if you let go of my hand halfway through?"

They both stopped, seeming to have the same thought at the same moment. Would it cut her in half? "Gross."

"Yeah."

They continued up the winding sidewalk, beneath the tentacle-like branches of a twisty old tree and Vanessa put the collar of her jacket up. The weather was cooler inside Midnight Villas, as if it were perpetually autumn.

"You did notice that the sidewalk is made up of old gravestones?"

Mina nodded. "Yeah, I was just hoping *you* wouldn't notice. It's creepy, but on the other hand, it is recycling…"

They both laughed, but Vanessa was obviously tense and Mina worried that the whole thing was freaking her out more than she let on.

"There's the UFO," Mina said as they crested the hill and were suddenly bathed in a green glow—the same green glow that had emanated from the phone just the other night.

They headed up the walkway.

A hatch on the smooth, silver side of the spaceship opened and a gangplank lowered down. Darkness filled the inside of the ship. Mina took a step forward and noticed that Vanessa wasn't following her.

"I'll wait here."

Mina rolled her eyes and sighed. "You're just going to stand there while I go in by myself?"

"Uh huh. I'm just the sidekick. This is totally your gig."
Mina huffed.

She turned and stared up into the UFO. It was fine to

think about meeting alien beings, but now that she was here, she was finding it a lot harder. Each pet sitting job was another step toward Zoo Camp, though. She took a deep breath and bounded up the gangplank.

If Midnight Villas was chilly, the inside of the ship was exactly the opposite. It felt like a jungle. Somewhere something was dripping and the floor sloshed beneath her sneakers. "Hello?" In the dark, she heard the sound of an enormous snake slithering across the wet, metal floor. Another snake sound joined the first and then suddenly if sounded like a dozen snakes inching toward her.

She gulped. "Uh…"

Something kind of slimy wrapped around her hand and she almost screamed. It was a tentacle, not a snake. That didn't make it any, better though. Mina froze with fear.

"Human," a voice said, but it was inside her head, not in her ears.

"Uh…"

The tentacle moved and it gently shook her hand. "Greetings human female," the voice in her head said.

"Uh…"

"How rude I am," the alien said. "You can't see in the dark." She heard the slithering sound again and a switch was clicked. A bank of overhead lights flickered to life.

Mina wished they hadn't.

The alien was taller than her, but not by much, its body a heap of green flesh resting on a tangled mess of tentacles that writhed beneath it. A dozen eyes blinked at her.

She clamped her hand over her mouth to keep from screaming.

The creature's enormous slime-filled mouth twisted up in a smile. "That's better."

"Uh…yeah. Much. Thank you."

"This craft is departing this celestial body for a time-span of three planetary rotations and require a custodian for my familial lesser creature."

Mina nodded. "You want me to watch your pet for a few days?"

"Precisely, human female. You are as intelligent as Count Dracula communicated to myself."

Mina smiled, glancing around the inside of the spaceship. She didn't see any pets. What kind of pet would an alien have, anyway? Space dog?

The alien reached into its mouth, pulled out a small blob of gunk and dropped it at her feet. Slime splashed up onto her sneakers.

Mina opened her mouth to speak, but couldn't find the words.

The alien's tentacles wiped the saliva off the blob, scooped it to hand it to her and smiled proudly.

"Uh…" Mina cringed but then took the basket-ball

sized blob in her arms. She expected it to be cold and slimy, but it was actually warm and slimy. She couldn't decide if that was better or worse.

"So, what does, uh, it eat?"

The alien touched its own head with one tentacle and then touched Mina's head with another. She cringed again at the cool, slimy feeling. But then light flashed in her memory and she suddenly knew everything she needed to know about taking care of the creature. Wow, total brain download. She wondered if she could learn math that way. That would be helpful.

The spaceship rose beneath her feet. It was time to go.

Mina waved to the alien and walked back down the ramp to the ground. The spaceship wasted no time retracting the ramp, ascending into the air and disappearing into the darkening sky.

Mina stood next to Vanessa, watching until the green glow was gone.

Vanessa took one look at the shapeless creature. "Nice mucus."

"Be nice," Mina said, petting the thing. "You're a little cutie, aren't you?"

"You realize you're probably talking to his butt, right?"

Mina shrugged, searching her brain download for where its butt was. It had to be in there somewhere, didn't it?

Vanessa made a face as she stared at it. "What does it eat? Where is it going to sleep? How are you going to do this?"

Mina was still searching her memory, trying to figure out how to remember what the alien had shown her. But, she also wanted to appear professional.

"Don't worry, pet sitting is *my gig*, remember? Besides, how hard could it be?"

ACKNOWLEDGEMENTS

Special thanks goes to a number of people who helped bring this book to life: my original publisher Miles Boothe, and to editor extraordinaire Barbara Ann Watson. To Peggy Mix, who put a pencil and Ray Bradbury in my hand, and to my mom who taught me to dream. And most of all, to my wife Melissa who is my dream come true, who helped me reach this dream and who reads all of my stuff and still laughs at the funny bits.

ABOUT THE AUTHOR

Gary Buettner haunts the suburbs of Northern Indiana with his family. He writes spooky monster stories and loves to hear from his readers at www.monsterpetsbooks.com.

Made in the USA
Monee, IL
07 May 2021